Best Date Ever

Best Date Ever

TRUE STORIES
THAT CELEBRATE
Gay Relationships

EDITED BY
LAWRENCE SCHIMEL

alyson books
NEW YORK

Manufactured in the United States of America.

This trade paperback original is published by
Alyson Books
P.O. Box 1253
Old Chelsea Station
New York, New York 10113-1251

Distribution in the United Kingdom by
Turnaround Publisher Services Ltd.
Unit 3, Olympia Trading Estate
Coburg Road, Wood Green
London N22 6TZ England

First edition: April 2007

07 08 09 00 🄰 10 9 8 7 6 5 4 3 2 1

ISBN 1-59350-008-4
ISBN-13 978-1-59350-008-4

Library of Congress Cataloging-in-Publication Data is on file.

CONTENTS

MEMORABLE MOMENTS

TRAVELS TOGETHER

TURBULENT TIMES

FAREWELLS

INTRODUCTION

SHARING THE MAGIC AND THE WONDER

LAWRENCE SCHIMEL

AN INTRODUCTION FOR an anthology is sort of like trying to set up a blind date. As anthologist, I am playing matchmaker, trying to bring potential dates (i.e. stories) to the attention of the reader, in the hope that they "click" and have an enjoyable time together. As with dating, not every encounter with every man will produce the right chemistry, but hopefully an enjoyable-enough time can be had by both parties, even if that spark is missing. Sometimes, some readers will find some stories not to their taste; one of the nice things about reading an anthology, as opposed to being out on a date that turns out to be a dud, is that it's easier to skip to the next piece than it is to walk out on a date-gone-wrong.

And while many of us have found ourselves on plenty of dates gone wrong, and there are many collections of worst date stories, this anthology sets out to do something different. We wanted to celebrate the romance of gay life, instead of always focusing on the negative; often, we spend so much time telling one another about an ideal man we feel is beyond our reach, the man who got away, the right situation with the wrong guy, or any of hundreds of other stories all-too-common in gay dating life.

In *Best Date Ever*, you'll find real stories from real men, sharing some of their most romantic moments and celebrating the wonder and the magic of intimacy between men. Whether a memorable first date or a special anniversary celebration, these personal essays offer glimpses of love at all stages of relationships, from the sparks of their first kindling to the warm glow of banked coals.

Sometimes our most romantic moments turn out to be with men who do not remain in our lives, for whatever reasons, the ephemeral nature of the encounter heightening the romance of the moment. Other times, those men are a daily constant we never take for granted, even many years later, and we find romance and tenderness in the small details, not just the major occasions. Whether fleeting or lasting a lifetime, these relationships have a tremendous impact on our hearts and minds.

Some of the potential contributors to this volume had some confusion as to what constituted a date. Some mistook best date to mean "memorable fuck," and while sex is certainly a part of most of our intimate and sentimental relationships, it is much richer when accompanied or informed by the extra-sexual relationship that imbues these acts with deeper meaning.

Many writers I approached replied that they had never dated; they met their partner ages ago and that was that. So many of them didn't grasp how our lives and relationships are filled with dates of all sorts, not just first dates: the kind of stories we're used to hearing (and recounting) when we show our scars from the battlefields of singledom. (And in the modern and plural world of today's relationships, some men date even when in relationships with other men, adding to the complexity of our search for—and finding—romance and intimacy.)

There's no denying that relationships are hard, and require effort to maintain, not to mention the effort required to find one. Dating is exhausting (and often confusing), spending all that energy in search of that special someone, a companion who, for however long, fulfills some need in us. And even when in a relationship, it requires constant care and nurturing to keep it from growing stale.

Herein you'll find stories about the rewarding moments that

some men have found in their own dating and relationship experiences: accounts that are frank, inspiring, sometimes funny, always heartwarming.

I hope you enjoy your time together, and that, as readers, you feel that special click with one or many of these special tales of the wonder and magic of gay relationships that these men have been willing to share.

FIRST
MEETINGS

THE FIRST WALTZ

PHILIP CLARK

ALL MY CONCENTRATION was directed toward following his neck, his shoulders, the back of his head as our clutch of friends drifted across campus toward the University Center. He walked two steps in front of me, looking even thinner and paler than normal in the deepening dusk. Trying to will his attention toward me, I pulled up alongside as we shuffled closer to our destination. Tonight was, I had convinced myself, the best time to tell him how I felt. The necessary time.

Only our group's joking and excited talk broke the muted gloom of a Williamsburg evening as we approached the Sunken Gardens, the narrow terraced meadow that Thomas Jefferson had designed for our college. But when the University Center's staid brick façade came into view, we saw clusters of students gathered outside it. Noisy laughter from the crowds and an occasional sharp shout of recognition reached our ears. A last look at him before we arrived caused my stomach to churn with nervousness. This seemed to be the beginning of a stressful night.

A conservative campus, the College of William & Mary rarely cut loose, but Drag Ball was an exception. Gay and straight, students dressed in robes and frocks as elaborate as their money and imagination could devise. In bangles and sequins, purple feather boas trailing in their wakes, girls dragged their dates up to the sliding glass doors; while these boys made a show of protest, scuffling their feet against the ubiquitous brick walkways, their eyes betrayed their curiosity as they drank in the scene.

Word of the party had spread to the cities near Williamsburg, our combination college town and tourist trap. Gay boys from Virginia Beach, Norfolk, and Newport News had hopped rides to join with the students. Professional drag queens had been hired from Richmond, arriving in floor-length gowns slit up the thigh, their hair teased into glamorous towers. Despite warnings from testy school administrators, worried that news would leak to Williamsburg's right-wing local press, a few of the hornier male members of the Gay Student Union had even pitched in to hire strippers as a blowout for the evening. The resulting mix created an atmosphere of general giddiness.

Midway through the event, though, Drag Ball had been just that: a drag. Despite its billing, there hadn't even been dancing. The lowered lights and pulsating strobes seemed a recipe for energy and movement, but instead everyone milled about uncertainly, waiting for something to happen. I looked around at the gathered crowd, annoyed that not one of them was daring enough to be the first exposed to others' eyes on the empty dance floor. Then again, neither was I.

But I needed to be. After all, there he was beside me, standing close enough that I could feel warmth radiating from his arms and back. I saw him smile happily as throbbing techno gave way to drag divas fake-belting their lip-synched notes. Framed by his hair's soft black spikes and the sparse and bristly goatee he had just begun to grow, his face glowed in this weird, half-lit world.

I was a junior, he a freshman, and we had been shyly courting for the past few months without it ever being a date. Out to the delis that passed as Williamsburg's bars and nightlife; off to movies that the Film Society screened so seriously; away for milkshakes at Lodge One, the late night on-campus hangout. We were always in groups, but did he notice that he was the only one I saw? Whenever I spoke, now matter who I was addressing, it was always directed at him—wanting to impress, not to mention to avoid saying anything to risk losing what I hoped could be his love. I began to believe that, when he looked at me, he felt the same way. But like our classmates at the ball, we scratched around the edges of the floor, neither of us willing to plunge forward and risk exposure. I had half-convinced myself that, if I could ask him to dance, I could reveal how I felt without even needing words.

This, though, was not the place. Movement on stage snapped me away from my thoughts. The drag queens had given way to a nearly naked stripper, hips wriggling in time to the beat. The stripper writhed to his knees, arms akimbo. It was hard to see in the dim light, with students crowding in for a better view, but the glint of metal flashed in his palm. A tall, painfully thin drag queen strode forward. She slid the cuffs from the boy's hand, then snapped them once, twice on his waiting wrists.

This wasn't what the evening was supposed to be. It seemed a good time to leave. Not wanting to yell above the music, I leaned down to speak into his ear: "I don't know about this. Do you want to take a walk?"

He smiled at me nervously. "Sure, we can go."

We walked the central spiral staircase in the University Center, passing wide-eyed girls covered in glitter and two boys having an argument. "I hate this!" one said. "I never wanted to come." He shied away as we passed them, looking embarrassed for their public fight.

Outside was a different world. Our ears still rang after the thumping of the dance music, but the night was sharply silent. It was mid-February, the air crisp, but not so cold that our jeans and T-shirts weren't enough. We walked closely, without touching, through the center of Old Campus, passing beside a weeping willow and beneath the elms that shadowed the brick walks. Who could remember what we talked about? Pleasantries. Our minds were elsewhere. The bulk of the Wren Building loomed ahead of us, its three-hundred-year-old chapel and classrooms darkened. The meandering paths led us to the cast-iron statue of Lord Botetourt and beyond to the historic district.

I never spent time in Colonial Williamsburg during the day.

Even though I was a junior, I hadn't gone through any part of it more than two or three times in daylight. Masses of tourists, their screaming children in tow, made the experience an unpleasant one. At night, though, it turned magical. The tourists dissipated, the workers in colonial costume retreated behind closed doors, and stars appeared, clear beacons above the chimneys and gabled rooftops. But our silent walk was making me anxious, unsure whether leaving the campus had been a good idea. With his quiet presence at my side, my mind cast itself outward, searching for how to ask what I wanted, trying to come up with a plan. I don't know what made me think of the Governor's Palace, but when it entered my thoughts, I knew what we could do. "I think the Governor's Palace is nearby," I told him, trying to seem confident and knowledgeable about where we were. "Do you want to jump the wall?"

At any college, there are traditions. At one as old as William & Mary, tradition takes on a force, the weight of history. In modern days, there are three tasks that every student is said to have to complete before he can graduate, and this triathlon is drilled into every freshman's head:

You must swim through the Crim Dell, a picturesque campus pond.

You must go streaking through the Sunken Gardens, the meadow designed by Thomas Jefferson.

And you must jump the wall of the Governor's Palace, find the colonial-era maze within, and work your way to the center.

Of course, all these activities carried with them varying degrees of illegality, going against, as they did, such social niceties as not trespassing or being naked in public. The campus cops and Colonial Williamsburg police were said to be generally lenient with those offenders they caught; still, the specter of potential arrest hung over anyone who attempted the trifecta. In one silly, glorious night my first year at the school, some friends and I broke through our mid-year lethargy long enough to do all three. But, as I suspected, he had yet to try any. A freshman and still somewhat law-abiding, he hadn't had the time or inclination. I could see his hesitation, but he smiled just the same and said, "We can do anything you want to do."

I knew then that if I could ever get up the courage to ask him out more formally than this late-night stroll through the deserted town, he would agree. Still, I couldn't speak. Why is it so difficult to ask that question, even when we know the answer will be yes?

We continued to wander, and to my embarrassment, I had no idea which way to guide us. Nearly three years of avoiding the colonial area or going there only in groups left me at a loss when I was in the lead. "I think the Governor's Palace is at the end of Duke of Gloucester Street," I said, hoping that he might know and step in. No such luck. "That sounds right," he replied tentatively. On we strayed through the night. Only stars and a few scattered streetlamps lit the way. In their spidery light, his pale skin and the deep black of his hair made him look like a figure stepped from an Aubrey Beardsley drawing, all whites and darks. He looked as perfect as I had ever seen anyone.

My navigational skills were not so perfect. The Governor's Palace was not at the end of Duke of Gloucester Street. There was a wall ahead, but much lower than the one in my memories. We decided this must be the Capitol. "I guess I don't know where I'm going," I apologized. I feared I was screwing this whole thing up, making matters worse, but he reassured me. "It's okay," he said, "we can just keep walking. Don't worry. We'll find it."

On we went, down a gravel trail at the edge of the Capitol, holding onto the rickety wooden rail beside it. To my surprise, being lost opened us up. We already knew the basic details. But as we floated through the empty town, running across buildings we'd never seen ("God, that purple clapboard is hideous!") and places we'd never heard of ("There's a golf course back here! Where the hell *are* we?"), there was nothing to do but laugh at our situation and tell each other those stories that would reveal the people we had been prior to meeting. I told of a quiet growing up outside of Washington, D.C., family trips to New England and my aunt's house on Cape Cod, how I wanted to be a writer. He was from a farm near Richmond, then, after his parents' divorce, the rolling hills in the Blue Ridge, deep in southwestern Virginia. He had known for years that he wanted to be an elementary school teacher; both his mom and sister were. His sister had gone to Emory & Henry, a tiny college near home in Appalachia, and his mom had hoped he would go there, too. "But I wanted William & Mary since I was a little kid, when I took a trip to Colonial Williamsburg. I remember some of these places from when I first visited. I knew I had to come here."

"I'm really glad you did."

"So am I," he said. "I'm glad to be here."

"I mean, we never would have met if you hadn't."

He smiled at me. "Yes, that's true."

And that was how it went, searching for some sign of which way would return us to campus, when there it was. We both stared to our right, down the expanse of lawn lined with catalpa trees leading to the Governor's Palace.

"Do you still want to?" I asked.

Nervousness again. Hesitation. "If *you* want to . . ."

"Let's do it."

We stole like petty thieves across the manicured grass, partners in crime planning our break-in. The first time I had done this, as a freshman, someone left the gate unlocked, but we weren't as lucky. This was okay, though. No one makes it easy on two boys to do what they want together, and besides, it would have defeated the purpose. We were supposed to go over the wall, not profit from the mistake of some overworked palace employee.

We found a lower section of wall, away from the main gate and the eyes of passing police. A glance, a gathering of our strength, a jump and quick struggle to scale the worn bricks. It was lucky that neither of us had gone to the ball in drag. That kind of athletic feat would then have been indecent in addition to illegal. But we both made it and dropped safely down to the grass and leaves quilting the palace grounds. It was even darker inside the wall than in the main town, and we took a minute for our eyes to adjust to the murky tones. Gradually, glowing stars lit the scene, and we could see oaks, ivy, vast empty earthen beds waiting for their springtime flowers. The moon appeared, a golden orb amidst the floating clouds, disappeared, and appeared again. A single lamp shone far up in the cupola crowning the palace roof. Just as lost as before, we let our feet guide us aimlessly through the empty garden.

"Are we supposed to find the maze?" he whispered.

"Sure, let's look for it."

We curved along the winding paths. "See the moon?" I asked. "When it's full like tonight, you can see a man's face peering down."

He squinted up into the sky. The clouds parted long enough for a clear view. "I'd heard about that," he said, "but I'd never thought to look. I'd never seen what they meant before tonight."

"It's beautiful here."

"It is."

We smiled again and shared another nervous laugh. Through the doorway of an interior wall, we could see hedgerows. Walking toward them, they were smaller than my imagination had conjured. Both of us were easily tall enough to see over the tops of the bushes and into the heart of the maze. "Oh," I exclaimed. "This will be simple."

Maybe this just wasn't my night. We slid along the maze's corridors, eyes peeled for likely turns, becoming more confused with every change in direction. Neither of us, it turned out, was good at taking charge and making decisions. Every time we reached another fork in the road, we giggled and stood amazed at how such a small maze could yield so many challenges.

"You decide this time."

I teased him back. "I've decided three times in a row!"

"Maybe we'd better just alternate."

"I guess we'd better. Keep it simple."

Each minute felt like hours, our ears straining to catch any sign of a roving police officer inside the confines of the walls.

Somehow, our patchwork of decisions got us close to the middle of the tangle. Maybe by then we lost patience, or maybe we felt incapable of reaching the center, but I found myself pushing prickly branches aside for him to plunge through the final layer of hedges.

"Don't step on the flowers," he warned.

"Yeah, just because we're cheating doesn't mean we have to kill things, too."

I followed quickly, and we were there. We had broken rules and roamed all over the sleeping town to reach our goal. But having reached this destination, did I have any better idea how to proceed?

"We made it."

"Yes, we did." He looked at me expectantly, yet still I could not speak.

We sat on a convenient bench, glad to rest our legs, and craned our necks upward. Late winter breezes blew the clouds endlessly, and the moon continued its vanishing act above our heads. At moments, he almost disappeared into the darkness. Then the shade would lift and I could see the gentle slope of his shoulders, the soft shine in his eyes, cheeks reddened from the wind.

"Can I ask you something?"

"Anything you'd like."

Even with this open invitation, the words would not come. I stood up suddenly, angry with myself. I turned to look at him, sitting, waiting for my question. What came out was, "Have you ever waltzed before?"

What the hell was I doing? He looked at me quizzically. "Have I *what*?" he asked, laughing. But when I beckoned, he came to me.

For whatever reason, despite the ridiculousness of what I was asking, I felt oddly calm. "Would you like to?" I asked. "I mean, would you like to try?"

He grinned at me. "Yes," he said, and I knew that he meant yes to everything.

If a policeman had arrived then, he would have seen us, hands on shoulders and backs, stumble through our very first waltz. The two of us, waltzing amid the hedges, beside the palace, underneath the stars and clouds and moon.

UP ON THE ROOF

FRANÇOIS PENEAUD

I NEVER THOUGHT I'd get that romantic date that fills movies and novels, the one you remember for the rest of your life. I was just out of a relationship that had been part good sex and part good exercise for the lungs: usually we'd shout at each other for a while and then make love. It was invigorating for a while, especially since it was the first relationship for both of us, but I was hoping for something less nerve-wracking.

Only a few days after that breakup, here I was, in the flat of a man I already considered a friend, and I kind of knew something would happen, without really wishing for it. I was a bespectacled student about to pass my math teacher exams, and I looked even younger than I was. That's not supposed to be a self-inflicted compliment—I was really still wet behind the ears. Michel was an amiable, mustachioed man, and he was fifteen years my senior. I never looked at guys over thirty or with facial hair in those days, but I think I was already under his spell, maybe because he was so different from the few other gay guys I knew, even if I definitely wasn't in love with him.

We'd met only fourteen days before, under rather unusual conditions for me. Three days shy of my twenty-sixth birthday, I went to a meeting to prepare what would be the first gay pride celebration in Toulouse, my hometown. I'd heard of the meeting a few days before, at the screening of a gay film at a local independent theater. I'd decided to go, even if my then-boyfriend wasn't interested. Yeah, I was still with the guy at the time, and was trying to find the courage to break up.

Why did I go? I wasn't part of any gay group, and I'd come out to my family only a few months before. I guess I thought it was time to get involved in gay activism, and maybe meet more gay people—not for sex (was I being honest to myself there?), but mainly to meet people. And in walked Michel, with a friend of his who I assumed was his boyfriend (you know, two gay guys walking in together, what else could it be? Told you I was green.). I found myself staring at him for the whole meeting. Ohh, a gay guy over thirty. And he seemed intelligent and even-tempered (so, only one thing in common with me, I'll let you guess which one) I had to find a way to talk to him; intellectual curiosity and all that.

We hit it off quickly and met often during the following week, for the pride planning meetings or when we distributed leaflets to gay bars. He even bought me a drink for my birthday, and I began to trust him and told him all about my current, fascinating life. I was so absorbed in my own drama that it never occurred to me that he was beginning to be attracted to me. Maybe because I couldn't imagine a guy like that being interested in me. Did I mention he had large shoulders, large arms, and a really nice smile? Of course, the way he behaved around me the next Saturday at that gay nightclub, when he put his arm around my shoulders, should have made me think we were already past the friends stage, at least for him. As I said, I had huge emotional blinders on.

Let's skip forward another week. I'm standing at the entrance of the fifteen-story building where he lives, having been invited for dinner. It wasn't even officially a date, but as clueless as I was, I still felt nervous.

His flat was a real Aladdin's cave for me: full of books, tapes, and CDs. That really impressed me, as his cultured ways had already impressed me. We all have our turn-ons, and I guess the fact that someone can teach me things and engage my mind was one of mine (don't worry, I also have other, more physical, turn ons.) What did we talk about? Literature, films, and foreign languages, his great domain of knowledge, which impressed me even further. Mathematics may be a language I know well, but it isn't that useful for communicating with people; not like, say, the European languages that Michel could use more or less well in a conversation. I wasn't in shock—yet—but I was already in awe of that guy.

The dinner went well. He had prepared salmon and pasta—and the pasta was overcooked (which became a tired joke between us for years). I must admit, I was half-awaiting some kind of "serious talk" to happen, but all the same, Michel was about to surprise me in a big way.

His building had a flat roof, accessed via a small stairway above the fifteenth floor that led to a door for which all the residents had a key. The door opened onto the roof itself, and from time to time people went up there; for example, to watch the fireworks on Bastille Day. It was around midnight, and Michel told me I should see the view from that roof, that it was really something—even nicer than the view from his fourth-floor balcony. On that May evening, it wasn't cold anymore, but a thin wind was blowing and, yes, the view was wonderful. We walked to the edge of the roof, which was enclosed by a man-high cement fence.

Toulouse is called the Pink City not because of its gay population, which is sizeable, but because of the traditional brick used to build its older edifices. It's quite beautiful, and when the sun is setting, the effect can be magical. But of course, it was a bit late for that, even though the urban lights created a field of stars as far as the eye could see (okay, first and last attempt at a poetic image. Promise.). We were on one of the highest buildings of the area and, since most buildings around here are at most four or five stories high, nothing prevented us from seeing far and wide.

Michel pointed out the best-known landmarks. And then, he switched to more personal matters.

"So, I need to tell you something," he said in a subdued voice.

I was slightly trembling, but not because of the wind.

"Yes, what about?" I asked, acting as though I had no clue.

"Well, we haven't known each other for long, but . . ."

"But . . .?"

"But I already like you."

"Oh, I like you too," I said, and I was completely sincere.

"I mean, I really like you," he said, beating around the bush.

"Well . . . me, too," I answered—apparently, the bush was either deaf or stupid. Or both. Or cold? Right, that's it. The wind had shut down all my neurons.

"Okay, let's try again: I've got to tell you this, even if . . ." He didn't finish that sentence, but took a deep breath, and plunged headfirst into the cold, cold waters of the unknown. (Damn. I'd promised I wouldn't try another poetic image.)

"I-I think I've fallen in love with you." There, he'd said it. My eyes grew wide. I'd been expecting something like this, but to hear it . . . I had absolutely no idea how to react, but I knew one thing: I didn't want to hurt him.

"Oh." And the prize for Best Answer of the Year goes to . . . me.

"Look, I'll totally understand if you tell me you don't want to see me again, or that you're interested in Marc or . . . But I had to tell you, tonight."

Marc . . . I haven't told you about him yet. During that first planning meeting for the gay pride celebration a student talked about the new gay and lesbian group they'd set up at the humanities university. It wasn't surprising that I hadn't heard of it—the math university wasn't known for its openness toward gay students.

I went to a meeting of the student group, and there I'd met a few nice people around my age, among them Marc, a guy with a nice sense of humor and an interest in Jean Genet, which I shared. He'd been with me at that gay club when Michel had tried unsuccessfully to put the moves on me. I was still too raw from my breakup, and I'd left with Marc. However, neither Marc nor I were interested in each other. Marc was after a dark-haired hunk and I was after nobody at the time. Michel didn't know that, of course, and so he'd jumped to conclusions.

That night on the roof, I denied any attachment to Marc, at least beyond friendship. The funny thing is that Michel didn't really like Marc and later told me he found him cold.

"I don't know what to say. I'm not sure I'm ready for another relationship." I wasn't lying at all. I was a mess and it would take me weeks to regain some measure of stability. "As I said, I really like you, but . . . You know, if I pass my exams, it's very likely that I'll have to leave Toulouse to teach where I'll be sent," I added. What was I trying to do? Convince myself of the impossibility of falling for this man? Blame the Ministry of Education, which would give me a job somewhere else in France?

"Well, you said you probably won't pass those exams—that will give us another year," he answered, which sounded involuntarily cruel and left me without an answer. While I'd already passed the written exams, I hadn't prepared much for the orals still to come.

"But . . . how can you be in love with me in such a short time?" I asked, trying to make sense of what was happening. If only I could have used math and logic to analyze everything. Love . . . that's like complex numbers, isn't it? Something we talk about all day but doesn't even exist.

Nah, I wasn't jaded enough to believe that.

"That's a very good question, and I don't know," he said, with an honest smile.

"Brr! It's getting cold," I said, really shivering in my T-shirt.

He then did something I wasn't expecting. He hugged me tightly, stroking my back to warm me.

"Feel better?"

"Uh, yeah, I do." Resistance is futile, after all. I could smell him, and feel his cheek against mine.

"I-I want to be honest. I don't really know what I'm feeling right now." I had to make myself clear. "Could you . . . give me some time to think about it?"

"Sure, I'll be here," he answered. What was he thinking? Did he believe things would work out?

I turned toward the edge of the roof and looked at the town below us. I put my hands on the sill, watching the cars tracing arcs of light on the streets far below. Michel was still hugging me, his strong arms making me feel safe and, can I say loved? I'm sure I can.

I felt my eyes water. I used to cry for nothing during those weeks after my breakup, but that time, it wasn't for nothing. I savored the moment, wondering whether it was the beginning or the end of something.

We remained there for some time, without talking, just enjoying each other's warmth, then decided to get back to the flat.

It was about one o'clock, I think. I was exhausted, more emotionally than physically, but Michel was determined not to let me go.

"I was wondering. Would you like to spend the night?" he asked as we sat on the sofa.

Sex on a first date? That wasn't what I had in mind. And this wasn't even supposed to be a date! Only dinner with a friend.

"I-I'm not sure that's . . ." I stammered.

"I don't mean—I only thought—we could sleep together. Really sleep. We can keep some clothes on, if you feel like it," he said, making me look like a scared virgin not wanting to discover what men were all about.

Okay, that's what I was. A scared virgin at heart. But I agreed to stay the night.

We cuddled in bed, still wearing our underwear, Michel behaving like a perfect gentleman. As for me, I was wrecked between two men: the one I'd broken up with only days before, about whom I was feeling really guilty for abandoning (he had his own problems, but besides that, we just didn't get along); the other I was sharing a bed with right then, and who had done everything to make me feel at ease, and seemed like the kind of guy I could definitely fall for. But things worked out.

Soon after our night on the roof I was having lunch at my parents' home. I had decided to tell them about Michel, our budding relationship, and the fifteen-year gap between us, and I would never—ever—have been able to anticipate my father's reaction.

"Can he feed you if you fail the exams?"

His concern for me was completely practical, whereas I was expecting a lecture on morality. To be fair, we (meaning, my parents and I) were convinced I wouldn't pass those exams, but I had never intended to be a kept man. I wasn't cute enough for that. Michel wasn't rich enough, either.

I don't remember what I mumbled back, but then my father said something I'll never forget: "I've had only two wives in my life, you know," which, as far as I know, was true. He'd been married twice, and I don't think he'd met other women apart from his wives.

Anyway, imagine it: my father comparing my situation to his. He's a good man, but my *weltanschauung* and his don't have much in common, to say the least. He only officially knew about my being gay for about six months. I say "officially," because I'm sure they both knew some time before. Don't they always?

In my case, that's more than a mere probability, thanks to a letter from my previous boyfriend, which it seems I'd left open on my bed when I was still living at their place. The jury is still out on that one: did my parents unfold that letter, or did they only read it out of curiosity? Some family secrets are best left unexplored, I guess.

As it happened, Michel hasn't needed to provide for me. I passed those exams two months later and at the end of that summer, I left Toulouse for the first time in my adult life—for a few years. Our relationship survived, as unlikely as it seemed at first. But that's a story for another time.

We haven't been on that roof in years, but I think of it from time to time. We don't get into shouting matches, which is something I undeniably appreciate. I'm the one who has the short temper, and Michel is the one who remains calm (most of the time). That's enough to take the wind out of my sails.

And eleven years after our first non-date, we're still very much in love.

MOOSE!

ERIC ANDREWS-KATZ

"SHOW TUNES."

The words thundered to my ears. I might have still been a little stoned from a joint earlier in the evening, but over the pulsing music of the bar and the screamed conversation of its patrons, I thought I heard correctly. I had asked this handsome man I had just met, whom I only knew as Alan, a simple question. "What kind of music do you listen to?"

His needle-in-a-haystack answer hit dead on, freezing me in my tracks. With a coy and sheepishly embarrassed grin, he cast his eyes downward and leaned in to speak. "You're gonna run away now, aren't you?"

I stood in complete shock. If my brown hair were not already in a flattop-cut, it would have stood on end. My mouth hung open until I smiled wickedly, knowing my goatee would invoke impish images.

"It's your *lucky* day!" I said with a chortle.

His response was a curious mixture of excitement and hesitation. "Really?"

"Let's just say, when you look up 'show queen' in a slang dictionary, it's *my* picture giving you an ovation. It's my dirty little secret." I winked.

The grin on Alan's boy-next-door face widened. The blinking lights cast a multicolored glow across his clean-cut, apple-pie image. We appeared to be the same height, five feet ten inches, but his chest was much broader than my average build. He wore a long-sleeved white shirt, with the cuffs unbuttoned and rolled halfway up his forearms, and a white T-shirt underneath. As we resumed dancing, my inner voice summed up my impression: "He should be a good fuck for the night."

When the music changed we took a break and headed over to one of the side service bars. I wiped my hands on my blue jeans, then tugged on the long sleeves of my striped shirt, trying to cool myself down.

"Where's your friend?" Alan asked.

"I don't know." I was suddenly aware he was nowhere in sight. I dismissed him with a shrug. "Doesn't matter, I'll walk home."

"Is he your roommate?" The question was leading.

"Actually, he's the roommate of my ex-boyfriend. *That* ended amicably right before New Year's Eve, so I took it as a sign to start the new millennium; single and happy to be so."

"And how's that working out for you?" He leaned onto the bar, resting on one elbow; a playful interest aroused.

I held up an empty left hand. "Three weeks and no ring!"

"I'll drink to that." And we did.

"So I take it you're not with that guy you were dancing with?"

He looked shocked. "Oh, God, no! He was trying to pick me up when I saw you staring."

"Sorry to interrupt you."

Alan scoffed. "I wasn't interested in *him*."

"Then it's a lucky day for both of us." I raised my vodka cranberry to his and we clinked glasses. "Are you really a musical theater fan?"

Alan stood erect at full height, his brown hair crossing the top of his forehead. He blinked his eyes and slowed his grin. "I'm not a *huge* fan or anything."

I interrupted. "I am." My smile was contagious for I saw one appear almost immediately on his face.

A taller man, pear shaped and dressed in a leather vest over a white T-shirt, approached and stood next to Alan, waiting to be introduced.

"This is Eric," Alan said, after having presented me to his roommate.

"You're the Massage Guy," his roommate said.

"Do you know each other?" Alan asked.

"Not really," the roommate volunteered to my quizzical look. "I gave a boyfriend a ride to and from your office, for an appointment. We met briefly."

"Story of my life." The comment went ignored or unheard.

"How long have you been doing massage?" Alan asked.

"About eight years."

"Alan," the roommate interrupted again. "Sorry to say it, but we need to go. I have to be up early tomorrow."

An awkward pause hung in the air as heads turned toward one another, forming a triangle. Alan slowly faced me, his head cocked on angle as if first debating and then reaching a decision.

"I have to go." Even over the music, I heard the hint of disappointment. "A friend of mine just had a baby yesterday and I'm making her split-pea soup to kind of help out a little. It's in a Crock-Pot, but I need to put it in the fridge."

Wondering if this was an excuse, I cast a sideways glance at the roommate, expecting him to speak up and volunteer to do the chore. He did his best to avoid my eyes.

I finally offered. "I walked here but I can drive you home, later."

Alan's smile rewarded my answer. "You're sure? Ok. Thanks."

Good-byes were exchanged and the roommate disappeared. And then we were alone, in a room full of men. We stared at each other, trying not to look too hard as our smiles matched each other's. When I put my cocktail back down, I made sure to place it close to Alan's hand, allowing our fingers to touch. Fueled by the reflection in his eyes, I wondered how long it would take me to get him to my home before his.

"Want to go for a walk?" His eyes looked imploringly. "We can chat for a bit and I'll catch a cab. You don't need to drive me."

"How about if I walk with you and we worry about the cab later?" I wasn't ready yet to let him walk away. I always believed that clever repartee was the basis for excellent foreplay. This would give me time to prove it.

"Let me grab my jacket from coat check and we can go."

The usually biting January winds of Seattle seemed unusually tame that night. Frost was in the air, but a thickened layer of clouds kept in what little heat the city released, resulting in a comfortable cold instead of bitter chill. We stood on the corner in front of the club, allowing the subtle warmth of alcohol and good company to take effect.

"It'll be easier if we go to Pine and Broadway to catch a cab," Alan suggested, leading down the hill.

"Ok. I'll keep an eye out for one."

Alan's smile brightened his face. He walked slowly, with a small hitch.

"Do you want me to walk on the curb?" I suggested, nodding to the gait in his step.

"No," Alan said. "It's just a slight twist in my ankle. Besides, a gentleman always walks between his escort and the road."

"I'm not an escort."

"Good. I don't pay for things that I can get for free." He looked ahead smugly and continued his step.

"So you have a sense of humor."

"Why so surprised?"

"Well, most men don't seem to share my wit."

"I've never been one to be like 'most men'."

"That's saying something." I let the compliment settle. "You know what I do for work, but what about you?" Small talk came easily as we walked. My apartment was only half a mile away.

"I'm in school." A tone of pride and self-confidence entered his voice.

"Ambitious for . . . ." I stopped walking to study his face. "Thirty-three years old?" I put him one year older than myself.

"Close. I'm thirty-four and I'm going *back* to school, smartass."

"Ah," I said in a faux Asian accent. "It is better to be a smart ass, than a dumb prick."

Alan's smile crept up the edges of his lips. "And if you are what you eat, which are you?"

I found myself in a rare situation; at a total loss for words. As he stood facing me, his back to the street and a smug look proudly worn, I saw a cab drive by at an intersection behind.

"Well," I said after the cab was out of sight. "I guess you told me." We continued on our way with me feeling a slight vindication. "Do you read lot?" I asked in a bad segue.

"Constantly," he replied. "I usually don't go to bed without reading a chapter of something. What are you reading?"

I smiled at his presumption that I read with regularity. "Right now, I'm reading a collection of short stories. I've been really busy with work, so short stories are about all I have time for."

"Is it an anthology or a collection?"

"It's a collection of stories by Truman Capote. Have you read anything by him?"

"Years ago," Alan said, his tone implying his opinion.

"You didn't like his work?"

"I only read *In Cold Blood* and I'm just not a fan of the 'murder for entertainment' aspect that's associated with it."

"That's only one part," I defended. "If you knew what it was about, why did you read it?"

"My book club voted on it."

I tried to steal a look at Alan as we passed underneath a streetlamp. The boyish charm that I had first noticed seemed to have shifted to a more natural setting. I noticed more-adult grey flecks at his temples. His eyes were green and when he looked directly into mine, I felt color touching my cheeks. I hoped he'd think it was the air's chill. We came to the crosswalk where I would turn toward my apartment. Without comment we continued past.

"Capote's short stories are a different animal from his novels." I felt the need to defend one of my favorite authors. "He's a pompous writer who uses words to show off his intelligence, but he tells a good tale. With the short stories he doesn't have time to display his great French vocabulary as much." I smiled, conjuring the author's image in my mind. "He was an ego-centric queen; gossipy and demanding." I let out a heavy sigh dismissing the spirit. "We would have been *such* good friends."

Alan let out a small chuckle. "Have you ever seen that movie by Neil Simon, *Murder By Death*? Where Truman plays the host of a murder mystery?"

"That's the one with the take-offs of all the famous detectives?"

"Right!" Alan's face lit up. His boyish delight gave way to handsome features with a playful sparkle. "I love the scene where he's talking behind the mounted moose's head on the wall."

I stopped walking, caught up in the excited shared memory. "And the Charlie Chan character says, 'Cow on wall speak.' Then the head screams out—"

Our voices squealed in unscripted unison, each of us doing our best impersonation of the high-toned, nasally elfish voice of Truman Capote.

"'Moose! It's a moose, damn it!'"

The impressions turned into laughter, the sounds of our joy rolling down the street. Neither of us cared if passersby heard us or what they must have thought. Neither of us seemed to notice if they were there at all. Alan's affection for reading and knowledge of movies ignited a kindred flame between us. I undid the top of my coat's zipper, feeling the refreshing cold night brushing around my throat. I stood still, staring at him, trying to decide whether I should kiss him. Another orange cab pulled around the corner and I made up my mind.

I leaned in and was met half way. Our lips touched and pressed together without opening. I could hear his breath and feel it mix with mine. Reaching out to touch his shoulder, his arm trembled as I took hold. I flinched involuntarily when his hand went to my waist. Our lips parted but we kept close. I felt his body's heat and grew warm, surrounded by Seattle winter's cold. I looked over his shoulder to make sure the cab had disappeared.

I nearly choked when Alan whispered, "Why is it that you can never find a cab when you need one?"

"Do you need one? I told you I'd drive you home."

He gently tugged on my arm, leading me on another meandering stroll around the main intersections of Broadway Avenue. "If we see one before we get to your apartment, we'll deal with it then. Where do you live, anyway?"

I pointed over my shoulder. "About three blocks back that way."

His look was incredulous. "Why didn't you say anything?"

"Good company is hard to find. Good conversation harder." I gave his hand a squeeze. "And if there is one thing I *am* a snob about, it's good conversation."

As if on cue, a taxi pulled around the corner. To my disappointment, the vacancy light was on. Alan jumped off the curb, raising his arm and shouting for the cab. The driver pulled up and waited. Alan walked to the rear door.

"Thanks for the company," he started.

The awkward pause fell between us as we both waited for the other to say something more.

"Here." I fished my card from my wallet. "Give me a call."

"You going to give me a massage?" His implication was ambiguous.

"No," I sharply answered. "It's my only phone and hopefully you can think of another reason to call."

His smile spread across his face. "Okay," he nodded. He leaned and gave me a quick kiss goodnight, letting our lips touch and linger. I stopped him just before he closed the door.

"What made you answer 'show tunes'?"

"What?"

"In the bar. When we first met. I asked 'what kind of music do you like' and you answered 'show tunes'. If you're not that big a fan, why'd you say that?"

Alan's face blazed. His grin widened until his front teeth were showing. He looked up into my face, ready to answer, but then stopped to laugh at himself. Taking a deep breath, he answered, "Usually, it freaks guys out, being a stereotype and all. It's a defense mechanism and keeps people at a distance." His sheepish grin was boyishly attractive.

"Hate to tell ya," I said slowly. "That's gonna bite you in the ass."

"Well, I guess that makes us even, considering this is the third cab that's passed us and you didn't say a word." He swung his legs into the car and slammed the door. Winking safely from behind glass, he smiled as the taxi pulled away.

I waited until the cab was out of sight before lowering my waving hand. Still staring afterward, I remained motionless except to zip up my coat, suddenly feeling the cold. Putting my hands in my coat pockets, I started for home, humming as I went.

I was halfway home before I realized the song I was humming was Rodgers and Hammerstein's "A Cockeyed Optimist". That song has a strong effect on me; it fills me equally with inspiration and hesitation for the same personal reasons.

. . . . .

I STOOD LOOKING out at the kind of day most Seattleites don't like outsiders to know about. There were few clouds floating by welcoming brief shade to an otherwise blue, late July sky. A distant but clear Mount Rainer stood witness and the Seattle skyline served as a backdrop across the waters of Puget Sound. My eyes weren't on the city's sights as were most others: mine were on the backs of the seated guests.

Nervously, I looked away, glancing over the buffet table and the welcoming setting with embossed napkins. Centered across their white background was blue, metallic-looking lettering that clearly read:

MR. ALAN ANDREWS

MR. ERIC KATZ

JULY 26, 2003

And below, a little larger than the rest, the single word:

"MOOSE!"

Only a few of our intimate circle of friends knew the details of how we met. Most of the seated guests had no clue what "Moose!" meant when they saw the napkins, and an explanation would be inevitable. That wasn't a problem. In the three-and-a-half years of being a couple, the alternative meaning had become special and after all, this day was for us.

The lyrics of "Unexpected Song" from the Andrew Lloyd Webber musical *Song and Dance* hit the air. That was the cue for us to appear.

"Do you have butterflies?" Alan asked from behind me.

I turned around and he stood proudly smiling. His boyish charm shined bright. He wore a black shirt, opposite my dark teal, and we both wore beige linen pants for the outdoor ceremony.

"Feels more like Mothra," I answered. "But, they're playing our song."

"Isn't that from a different musical?" Alan replied with a wink. "What? I did know something about musicals before we met. Come on. Let's go." He turned to lead the way.

"One moment." I grabbed his arm. "You do understand that this is 'Thunderdome'?" His curious expression made me continue. "Two men enter, only one walks away."

Alan's face lit up with a broad, reassuring smile. He hugged me around the waist and gave me a kiss on the lips.

"You've made that very clear," he whispered with a soft chuckle. "Let's get married."

As we stood before both our biological and extended families,

Alan took my hands in his and we faced each other. Winning the private coin toss, he would say his vows first. I noticed his bottom lip begin to quiver and could feel his palms begin to sweat. He took a deep breath and with a trembling voice began to speak.

"Never did I think that the words 'show tunes' and 'moose' would change my life."

While everyone laughed at my proceeding reputation, I stood across from this incredibly handsome and wonderful man trying not to cry in public.

With a smile, I silently thanked the gods of fate for musical theater and Truman Capote.

THE INTERNET

THE BLOGGER BOI

RYAN FIELD

LIZA MINNELLI USED to perform a song about a thirty-three-year-old, unmarried girl named Shirley Devore, who literally had to travel around the world to meet the guy next door. Poor Shirley, living up on Riverside Drive with aging parents; still a virgin, and desperate for love. Entertaining and comedic, the song shows the unmeasured lengths to which single people will go in order to find the perfect partner. Never in a million years would I have imagined that I'd be able to relate to that song.

But one day last spring, a rainy Monday so cold and damp you would have thought it was December, I decided it was time to start dating again. I'd had an excellent weekend. On Friday afternoon I'd logged onto one of those "listing" Web sites, the ones where you can buy or sell anything from bed sheets to automobiles, where you can search for, or advertise, unusual jobs, and where you can meet a lover no matter what your sexual orientation. I clicked on "men seeking men", scrolled the simple black and white listings for a moment, and then clicked onto an ad that read "Horny 23 year old top guy in search of good looking bottom for fun. I can host." There was a color photo: thin, tanned, nude torso; loose fitting jeans unbuttoned to expose *everything*— strong, young legs spread wide in a slightly bow-legged stance. Just what I needed. I e-mailed him, sent a few provocative shots of my seductive thirty-year-old body, and we hooked up at his studio in the Village that night.

We wound up spending the entire weekend together, doing everything a horny twenty-three-year-old top and a good-looking bottom can possibly do. On Sunday evening as I walked out the door he said, "Thanks man, that was fun," as he stood there with bed-head, wearing wrinkled white boxer shorts, scratching his crotch as though we were standing in a locker room and I was just another one of his football buddies. And it suddenly occurred to me that I'd secretly wanted more than just a thank-you. Spending the entire weekend together had not been planned, but once we discovered the powerful sexual connection (and he discovered that I'd gladly submit to anything his naughty mind could imagine, including some weird kinks that consisted of six-inch pink leather high heels and a white feather boa) time seemed to get away from us.

So I asked, "Would you like to get together later this week for dinner?"

His expression went blank. "Hey, buddy," he said, running the palm of his left hand over his hair, unable to look me in the eye, his hairy right leg starting to twitch, "This was fun . . . you're great, like play dough in bed . . . but it was only fun and games. Don't want anything heavy right now, Dude."

I smiled. With my right hand I reached into the fly of his boxer shorts, and said, "It's just a date, not a marriage proposal, but that's cool, man. No need to explain. See ya."

But I thought he should have said, "Yes, I'd love to have dinner. Be nice to get to know you better."

During the walk back to my apartment in Chelsea I began to question my life; not putting it down, just ready for a change. I'd had enough casual sex, with empty endings leaving no hope for the future. It was all too simple: finding a man on the computer, exchanging dirty photos, blunt information on sexual preferences . . . and it all gets tired. I suddenly wanted to discuss my life with someone, to spend a normal evening with a guy who was interested in things other than pounding me into his mattress time and again. I just wasn't sure how I was going to go about it.

On Monday as I sat before the computer to begin a day's work, rain sheeting against the tall windows of my parlor floor apartment on 23rd Street, I decided I'd start going out to bars and clubs again. Not much fun, but at least you can meet people and have a conversation. As a freelance writer working from home, producing short stories and articles and anything else they asked me to write, I'd become so consumed with work I'd barely had time for friends let alone going to bars to meet men. And when I discovered the "listings"—and how simple it was to find really first-rate, anonymous sex—I had just stopped dating altogether without even realizing it. Though going to bars and clubs wasn't always the best way to get a date, at least it was a step in the right direction.

My assignment that day was to write a review for an international site that listed and reviewed almost every gay blog in the universe. Not the most challenging work I'd ever done, but I enjoyed reading the blogs and truly believed the entire concept was just coming into its own. My reviews were always kind, though not always honest. Most blogs were awful—no-talent, self-indulgent, quasi writers more interested in vanity than learning craft, informing the world with poorly written journals about mundane lives and banal experiences. Who really cares about Allen-the-blogger's blue-haired, fat-assed grandma, the canned peas and carrots they had for Thanksgiving dinner, and the painfully amateur impatiens garden in his suburban backyard? It often took more time to find a decent blog than it did to write a three-page review. But it paid a hundreds buck per review.

I got lucky that morning. A blog by a guy named Jason Patriot (I've changed his name for this essay) caught my eye. The first thing I noticed was that there were no hidden marketing ploys: no sexual ads with half-dressed models pushing porn sites along the right side. Instead, there was a long list of recommended reading, both fiction and non-fiction, that the blogger thought was excellent. All works by gay authors, both current and classic. On the left side of the simple white page were sections to click, in medium blue print, which neatly and simply divided the entire Web site into categories of interest—Writings, Photos, Friends, Family, Vacations and more—all the topics the blogger was willing to discuss about his gay life. And dead center, in large bold print against a beige background, was a dated journal. He discussed a recent business trip to L.A.; the leak in his overpriced New York apartment; a long, awkward Mother's Day weekend with "Mommie Dearest." Not terribly exciting events, but when you read between the lines (he had a gift with sarcasm and wit) you sensed there was a really cool guy working very hard to make his blog interesting.

Being the superficial asshole that I can often be, I immediately clicked the Photos section expecting to see cheesy shots of a middle-aged queen trying too hard to remain young by wearing tight jeans pulled up to his bellybutton, or the expected bathing suit shots as he stood with his other middle-aged friends on a beach in Provincetown. The Simon Cowell type: too much money and no taste. But what I found were well-photographed shots of an attractive guy in his late twenties who didn't seem quite comfortable with the camera. A defined, slim body, short sandy hair—a tough-guy look that bordered on male hustler. There were shots of Jason posing without his shirt, exposing a well-defined chest with neat, round pectoral muscles that popped like upside down tea cups. There were photos of him in shorts, walking through the park, exposing muscular legs covered with soft, brown fleece. And there was a photo where he was standing beneath a green umbrella, out in the rain, wearing a bulky red sweater and loose-fitting jeans trying hard to appear happy, as though his face were in pain. The smile was reluctant, beneath serious deep, blue eyes that suggested he'd rather be home reading a book. I liked that photo the best.

Without hesitating, I e-mailed him with the basic questions—*How long have you had the blog? Why did you start it?*—and informed him that I'd be writing a review of his blog. If he could also choose a photo to go along with the review, I'd appreciate it. I also mentioned, in depth (something I don't normally do), that I truly enjoyed reading his work and thought the entire site was spectacular. There seemed to be a force of hidden power screaming from his site. After all the awful blogs I'd read and reviewed, I meant every single word.

Surprisingly enough, an hour later he replied with answers to the questions I'd asked, thanked me for all the compliments, and then said I should choose the photo because he was very self-conscious about them and really didn't like having his picture taken. I thanked him for his prompt response, and told him I'd have no problem choosing a photo since I thought they were all very good, especially the one where he was standing in the rain with the green umbrella. I wanted to tell him that I thought they were all really hot, but I figured it wouldn't be very professional.

He replied a minute later, obviously at home working, saying he thought it was interesting that I liked the "green umbrella" photo, the one he called "the frog," and wanting to know if I was attending some big blogger breakfast in Central Park on Sunday, an event for bloggers to get to know each other. When I replied that I hadn't known about the event, he asked if I'd like to meet him there. Taken aback, wondering if he was asking me for a date, I replied that I'd love to meet him there to discuss his blog more thoroughly. To which he replied, making himself very clear, "I'd love to discuss the blog, but this is more like a date. So I can get to know you better." We set up a time and place to meet on the following Sunday morning. Since I already knew what he looked like from the blog, I figured it best to e-mail him a photo of me, just in case I wasn't his type. I sent a conservative shot of me wearing a black T-shirt, hands in the pockets of my jeans, standing next to the entrance of a stone-fronted pastry shop in Tuscany, which had been taken the previous summer during vacation. "Thanks, looking forward to meeting you," was all he replied.

On Sunday morning I dressed warmly: a heavy brown tweed blazer over a white button-down shirt, and comfortable jeans that didn't show bulge. It was a cool, bright day, with strong breezes coming from the distant ocean, a hint of salt water that reminded me of summer's end. I'd promised to meet Jason at nine sharp, and knowing from the blog that he was always cheerfully early for appointments (even the dentist) I didn't want to be late. Our planned meeting spot was a cement bench, near the stables, and just in case either of us had a problem we'd exchanged cell phone numbers. My paranoid suggestion; though I'd lived in the city for nine years I'd somehow managed to avoid Central Park almost completely. For me, the park was this big green mass, with trees and joggers and stone bridges that you had to cross in a taxi to get to the Upper West Side.

When I arrived at five minutes to nine, Jason was waiting patiently on the bench, his sandy blond head turned slightly to the right, his blue eyes fixed on a young mother in a green poncho helping her eight- or nine-year-old daughter climb astride a massive horse. The little girl was in expert riding clothes—brown hat, jodhpurs, and all.

"Jason?" I asked, hesitantly, in case I'd been mistaken.

He quickly stood. He was taller than I'd expected, about six feet even. "Yes. And you must be Ryan."

"Ah, yes," I replied, extending my right hand.

"You look just like the photo," he said. "It's nice to meet you."

I thanked him and returned the compliment (if that's what it was). Then I noticed how stunning his blue eyes were, staring into my own with such an honest, open gaze. He wore a waist-length navy jacket, a white mock turtleneck, and khaki slacks. The jacket was informal, but very expensive in a casual way. His shoes were rugged, reddish-brown leather half boots, perfect for long walks in the park.

He was about to say something, but turned suddenly toward the young mother in the green poncho. The little girl was finally on the horse, but now crying and begging, "Please, I don't want to ride. Please, I want to go home," while the mother patiently persuaded, "You'll be fine, darling, you'll be a natural."

"I'm not quite sure if that's a good thing or a bad thing," Jason stated. "It could be good, in that it encourages the child to over-come fears, but bad in that it forces her to do something that's completely foreign to her."

"I'm not sure," I responded, "but I think as long as the mother is positive, and loving, it certainly can't hurt any."

Jason smiled. "I like that. C'mon, let's walk over to this blogger breakfast and see what's up."

Though we both tried hard to enjoy the blogger event, after about an hour of dull conversation and many superficial hand-shakes with virtual strangers eyeballing us from head to toe (we were the only young guys there), Jason decided he'd had enough, especially after one fifty-year-old blogger from Pittsburgh, with fake hair and vinyl cowboy boots, decided it would be okay to place the palm of his great hairy hand on the small of my back as though he'd known me a lifetime. Actually, Jason seemed some-what jealous, and I wasn't sure if I liked that or not. I explained af-terward that, being blond and innocent-looking, older guys didn't have a problem being aggressive with me and that I'd learned to just handle it politely. Especially the ones with a few bucks; they thought they could impress me and overpower me. I'd learned to not take it seriously. But Jason said he thought the guy was just plain rude, and the he should have treated me with more respect.

We both finally admitted that we despised breakfast food, from bacon to eggs, and Jason suggested we leave. There was a place he thought I might like, where we could just sit and talk for as long as we wanted. He wouldn't tell me where; I had to trust him, and I'd like it.

As we walked through the paths toward the park's edge, I re-alized that talking with Jason wasn't like talking with the other guys I'd known. There were no awkward moments of silence, no forced conversation to fill the empty gaps. He wasn't constantly answering his cell phone or checking his e-mail on his BlackBerry. He didn't mention his gym or wave his Rolex in my face. The words he spoke were honest and real, nothing to impress or create the expectation of more to come. The body language was relaxed, arms spread widely, shoulders often shrugged, the palms of his wide hands exposed to the world. Actually, talking with Jason was comfortable and easy, as though I'd known him all my life. When he said something too serious, I usually replied with a silly comment. He seemed to appreciate my sense of humor, and I wasn't really trying to be funny.

When we reached the Plaza Hotel, Jason stopped walking. And then he smiled.

"What?" I asked.

"We're here," he said, shrugging his shoulders. "They have the best strawberries and cream ever. C'mon, let's go inside . . . you'll really like this."

I followed Jason into the lobby of the Plaza. I'd only been there once, for the wedding of a dear college friend, a raven-haired, banana heiress, whose family came from South America and spared no expense for their only daughter's wedding. I hadn't expected we'd be going to the Plaza, or anywhere else so expensive. Good thing I'd brought my credit card that morning.

We were seated carefully at a small table covered in starched, cream linen with matching napkins so sturdy and perfect they stood upon the simple place setting as though they had minds of their own. The walls were drenched in gilt, with carvings so intricate and ornate and outrageous you would have thought you'd been transported back in time.

"Good morning, Mr. Patriot," said a middle-aged waiter in a black tie and crisp white shirt, jet-black hair slicked back. "The usual?"

"Two, yes, Raymond," Jason said, his blue eyes sparkling with light, "and champagne."

"Yes, sir," said Raymond, so familiar, yet dignified.

"They seem to know you around here," I said to Jason, spreading the napkin across my lap. Normally I would have been self-conscious, furtively glancing at the other tables, worrying that they were staring at me. But with Jason it seemed as though we were the only two people in the room.

"I like strawberries and cream," he said, shrugging his shoulders innocently.

But I suspected there was more, something he wasn't telling me, so I folded my arms and sat back in my soft, cushioned French chair.

Jason smiled, and then leaned forward. "Look, I suppose I should tell you that I'm not poor. Actually, I have more money than I can ever spend in a lifetime. I don't lie on the blog. I just don't let everyone know I have more money than God."

He confided this to me, for the first time that day not looking me in the eye, as though he were ashamed. I'd once heard a saying: People born with money often spend a lifetime apologizing for it; whereas people who earn their own money spend the rest of their lives making other people apologize to them.

"Jason," I said, "I don't need to know the size of your bank account right now. I'm here because I really liked what I saw and read in your blog, and so far I've had a great time this morning. I'll admit I was worried, apprehensive, and insecure about meeting you, but I'm having a really good time. I like you. Sometimes it really is just that simple."

"It's just that when you have money, a lot of it, people are either turned off by it, or they are always trying to score something with you. You're never quite sure who is being sincere. I don't know, it's my one flaw," he joked.

"Only one flaw," I laughed, trying to keep the conversation light.

"Well, that and I'm a terrible control freak," he admitted. "I know it's a problem, and I'm always working on it, but a lot of guys don't seem able to handle it."

"To be honest," I said, "I'd sort of guessed that about you. The way you seem to take charge all the time."

"Well, to be honest," he joked, his soft lips now parted in a half smile, "I sort of guessed you like guys who take control."

He was correct in that, but I also needed him to understand that I was only allowing him the control because I genuinely liked him, that I thought he was intrinsically decent and quite innocent in a little boy way. But more than that, he had to understand that I wasn't interested in his money. I didn't have millions, but I certainly wasn't poor by any standard. If Jason Patriot had been just an average guy with an average income, as I had assumed in the beginning, I would have been just as interested.

So I replied, "I want to put this the right way, Jason. My allowing you so much control is a conscious decision . . . it's not unconscious. And it's my decision to do so. If you try controlling me in a way I *don't* appreciate, you'll be the first to know about it."

He laughed. "Now I'm worried."

"Why?"

"Maybe I should be the one who has to be careful."

"I'm just as harmless as you are," I replied, smiling flirtatiously. I felt like I'd met my match.

We ate our strawberries and cream from crystal bowls with silver spoons, drinking champagne in tall, slim stemware, and for the next two hours we talked and laughed. When he declared that his favorite movie was *Peggy Sue Got Married* and saw the nonplused expression on my face, he said he liked that movie because Peggy Sue had traveled back in time and was able to see all the people she had once loved and were now gone. He would have loved a chance to go back to 1985, when he was only thirteen, to visit his late grandfather one more time.

During the quickest two hours of my life, I memorized the details of his face: strong and angular, with a square chin that had a deep crevice dead center. His shoulders were broad and level, as though they could balance wide platters. I noticed how clumsy his large hand seemed holding the delicate champagne glass, the way those long, wide fingers seemed flustered by such a skeletal object. And I knew that if he were to touch the skin, lightly, on my forearm, with just the tip of a finger, I'd become instantly aroused.

When the check arrived and I made a gesture for it, Jason quickly reached forward and said, "Remember . . . I like control." But it was only his way of joking.

I smiled, with tongue in cheek, glancing at him with an expression that shouted, "Okay, little boy, I'll let you have your way this time. You can pay the check."

As we stood to leave, he said, "I'll walk you home."

"I'm shocked," I told him. "I was expecting you to say, 'C'mon upstairs to my apartment. I live in the penthouse.'"

"No," he laughed, "I'm not the type to live here . . . my mother lives upstairs. I'm downtown, in Chelsea."

"Me too," I said.

"Excellent," he replied. "Should we walk, or take a cab?"

"Let's walk." Though I suspected in my heart this was just the beginning of something wonderful, I was hesitant about it all ending. Walking would ensure another hour or so.

We continued talking as we walked back to Chelsea, Jason telling me all his plans and how he wanted his life to be. He had a law degree, and though he enjoyed blogging and writing, he was on the verge of opening a gay literary agency. So many literary agencies handled gay writers, but there weren't many who were specifically geared toward the gay writer or reader. Though he admired the author of "Brokeback Moutain," he somehow found it politely offensive for a woman to write about the experiences of gay men, and for straight actors to be hired to portray gay men in the film. He said you couldn't quite put your finger on it, but something was wrong about the whole thing. When I argued that the actors were excellent, and wasn't that what acting was all about, he replied with, "Look at it this way, could you imagine Reese Witherspoon, though she is an excellent actress and can play any role she wants to play, getting the lead role in *The Rosa Parks Life Story*? The African-American community, not to mention the rest of America, would go crazy. I think gay men and women deserve that kind of respect, too."

I couldn't disagree. Actually, I'd managed to create a niche as a gay freelance writer without a literary agent, submitting material to gay publishers and Web sites for payment. I'd published short stories, novels, erotica, and more never bothering to think about a literary agent, knowing it would only be a waste of time.

When we reached my brownstone I pointed and said, "Here we are."

Jason's eyes popped, and he pointed. "That building?"

"Yes. Why?"

"That's where I live ... top two floors," he said. "I own the building. I'm JP Enterprises. You're the parlor floor unit?"

"Yes, I'm on the bottom," I replied, then, realizing the double meaning, lowered my eyes.

But he laughed, with a wicked grin, knowing I'd just given myself away. "You want to come up for a quick drink?"

I hesitated. I didn't want this wonderful date to become another one night stand.

"Look," he said, "I wish I could say that it's 'only a drink' but I'll be honest. I'm dying to get to know you better, and I can't promise I won't try to get into your pants. I've been dying to rip your clothes off since I saw you walking toward me in the park this morning."

He was being honest. Jason couldn't be anything else; skipping around the issues was not part of his character.

"But that doesn't mean you're actually going to get into my pants, blogger boi," I told him, pretending to play hard to get.

However, when he placed the palm of his strong hand in the middle of my back, practically pushing me across the street toward the brownstone, we both knew I'd never be able to resist anything he said. As he led me into the building where we both lived I knew, deep in my heart, that whether our new relationship lasted a week or a lifetime, that Sunday would probably be one of the best days of my life.

YIN AND YANG

MARVIN WEBB

WE MET THROUGH Match.com. This was my ad:

ABOUT ME AND WHAT I'M LOOKING FOR
TITLE: Bring It

I've got a list of things I'm looking for and a list of things I'm looking to avoid, which would be fine if I didn't prefer people to lists. How about we chuck the lists and just get to know one another by talking and frolicking (biking around the city, having some heated discussion over a NY Times article, feeding each other spring rolls with great dipping sauce, or just taking an afternoon nap together)? Say what you feel, do what you mean, and KISS LIKE THE DEVIL. Bring it—I'm ready, willing, and able. I'm an old soul in a youthful body with the spirit of a kid. I work hard and play hard, but live for neither. I just live. I love people and the adventures they bring with them. I really just want to play and if something works out, fine. If not, at least we had a great play date— eh? Show me your world and I'll show you mine. Thanks for reading . . . be well.

He read. He responded:

JAN 13, NATURE BOY (YANG)
SUBJECT: best

Well, I can't feel your hair but I think your best feature is

your gorgeous eyes! Holy crap, dude, gotta love those eyes! At some point, I'd like to take you to Montauk on a nice, warm spring day and go horseback riding or hiking around. Did you know there're sand dunes here on Long Island? You sound like the fun person that I'm looking for to do adventurous stuff! And I'm not even talking about sex! I find that a person's personality is what attracts me more than physical char. but I have to say that I'm really pleased with what I see. So I wrinkle my nose at you, and stick out my tongue, and I'm going to start gently poking you in the ribs until we wind up in a fun wrestling match! Oh, and say good night.

Yang

I was confused. I looked over my profile and saw I had set my hair as my best attribute. SHIT! But before I did anything to mine I looked over his:

ABOUT ME AND WHAT I'M LOOKING FOR
TITLE: Nature Boy

I'm a fairly sensitive man with a seemingly tough exterior. Although I'm in the spotlight every day I rarely meet gay men. I like dancing at clubs but don't meet the right type of guy there. Not looking for a hookup! Friends first. I like to keep it real. As long as we can tell each other the truth then we can go from there. I am very levelheaded, cool even in the hot situations and you should be too. You also like thrills, adrenaline, as long as no one is getting hurt. You know the difference between right and wrong, and are willing to stand up for your beliefs whenever necessary. People like us enjoy every moment given, whether a sunrise or gentle rain, a good song on the radio or silence. Also enjoy helping friends reach their potential, pushing your partner to be more and better, and finding happiness in doing so. I'm looking for a MAN for real! I am colorblind when it comes to people.

This was cute. He was really cute. And he runs a nature center. What the fuck is a nature center? Hmmm. But he lives out on Long Island! Are you fucking kidding me? SHIT! But I went into this on-line dating thing thinking that I'd have a great time and meet some great people, maybe even the love of my life. He is a hottie though, but does he look like his picture? So many men don't.

I sent this back:

SUBJECT: ABOUT THE HAIR
Yang,
   Didn't even notice that detail. Great catch. I'll have to change that. It would be great to meet. Like your pro-file. I'm interested in getting to know exactly what it is you do. Sounds interesting to say the least. Me—not look-ing for a hookup either. Am quite busy this weekend as I have an old gal friend in town, then I head off to DC for a two-day hang out with two gal friends there. So, it's pretty much a gal-on-gal weekend. Fun and festive, but busy. I'll be back on Tuesday, so we can connect during the week. Just moved back from DC after 5 years there. Was in NYC be-fore that for 11 years. Family is in Colorado Springs, but grew up in Kansas City. Short story. Have a great day,
   Yin
   22-XXX-XXXX cell
   XXXXXXXXXXXX@hotmail.com

Nature Boy (Yang) responded right away:

   Yin, Enjoy the weekend . . . girls night out! LOL Talk to you when you get back. Keep on keepin' on! Also, your area code didn't come thru . . . and DC is 202 and NYC is 212 so I guess I could try both . . .
   Yang
   631.XXX.XXXX

The next week, I sent this:

SUBJECT: GOOD MORNIN' NATURE BOY (YANG)

Yang, I must say that you sparked my interest in you when you mentioned horses and Montauk. Love them both, but the former scare me. I consider them such a sacred animal, I'm not comfortable riding them. I find them brilliant and noble and amazing. But enough about my thoughts on horses. I survived the weekend. My gal friend took me to see the Color Purple musical. It was good and there's no time like spending it with an old friend. The laughs and great ideas never seem to stop. There's pushing and digging and asking each other profound questions and then more laughter. Love that. Then off for one day for another friend's birthday. Still owe him a present, he's a hard one to shop for. So I made it back and went to yoga last night. So where do we take it from here? Do you work weekends at the nature center? What's the best time to meet? Any night is good usually except Wed as I work in God's Love We Deliver. My way of giving back I guess. What about Sunday afternoon? Let me know. I'm pretty open. I look forward to it. Believe me, you have very much sparked my interest. Have a great day.

Yin

202-XXX-XXXX, got the area code this time! LOL

I thought I'd give him a run for his money and changed my best attribute on my profile to my butt. Well it is pretty damned good: gay men try to get into it and straight women always want to know how I got it. I sent another message:

SUBJECT: PS I CHANGED MY FEATURE!

What do you think? ;-)

Nature Boy (Yang) wrote back that same day:

SUBJECT: BUTT

OK, now you're just straight up teasing me! How am I going to test this!!!??? Like all good scientific methods, I'll test a hypothesis and start with good observations! LOL And if visual observations are insufficient then I might have to just grab me some of dat ass!!! You're such a brat . . . I love it!

Yang

I called and he was busy and had to call back as he was with a friend. The idea went through my little head—is he a drug dealer making deals out on Long Island? Is that why he has to call back? Or is he fucking some other guy, answering the phone, waiting for the next fuck, or fucking while answering the phone and such and such? My mind is way too fucking busy. WAY TOO FUCKING BUSY! He called back and said that he couldn't talk and that he would rather talk tomorrow.

January 18, I sent this:

SUBJECT: BUTT LOVER

Y,

You're very funny. I guess you were so excited about the butt that you lost your train of thinking/thought. You didn't even answer my question about wanting to meet on Sunday! LOL So funny that I had to call you. Anyway, I'll tell you more about my butt, since you seem to have such an interest . . . I have spent the last 15 years being a professional modern dancer. Raised in Kansas City, college in Omaha, then around Europe and North America on tour for a couple of years, then moved to NYC to really start dancing at age 24. Had a blast training and learning all I could about the art form and all that it has to offer. Learned a great many things about people, the world and myself. But—back to the butt—right. So, yes I have a dancer's butt. It's not a large butt. I come in a small tight package. My butt's not menacing and I don't have linebacker legs, but I can move mountains with my body and throw anyone around—bed, street, and to the floor. As for what I do now ... I have to save something for the date, right? LOL The Date! We're meeting at Café Rafaella @ 134 7th Ave. It's between West 10th Street and Charles. It's on the west side of the street and it's two blocks north of the Christopher Street subway (1 line). It's on the same side of the street as the Riviera Café. The fun begins @ 12! LOL Also, there will be no inspecting of the butt until a later time. LOL I look forward to meeting you and seeing what you are like. Crazed, I know. Don't worry. I like crazy. But, not insane. ;-) LOL Have a great day Y, Y

He called. I was giddy like a little schoolgirl. It was nice to speak to him. He has a nice voice and great energy. But of course things change when they are live, right? We only talked for a short time, recapping things that were already mentioned, past lovers, how long we've been online on Match. I told him he would be date number fifty. I began on Match.com at the end of April last year. Maybe I'd get to one hundred by this coming April. Of course, he wanted more of an explanation. He wanted to know if I had slept with all of them. I told him no. But I did let him know that most men have had my cock (thousands, within the scope of Match.com and way fucking before!), but few have had my ass (six). I have to save something, right? LOL

The next day, Nature Boy (Yang) sent this:

SUBJECT: CALL

Ying, it was great speaking with you and being able to put a voice with a face! Can't wait to meet you! Ended up staying home last night instead of going to see that new movie with Queen Latifah ... feeling like a cold is trying to take hold. Going to cancel plans tonight too ... still not feeling 100% and now my throat is scratchy this morning.

Ugh. I don't have time for this. Were you ever an Ailey dancer? I always treat myself every year to an Ailey performance, except I missed this year … went to Puerto Rico instead. And just so you know, I like to joke around a lot, even flirt a lot … but I am always a gentleman first, and I NEVER have sex on the first date, or usually not even the second or third! I have to have a physical and emotional attraction b4 any barriers are broken! I guess I'm old fashioned that way. So I have some real motivation to get back to 100% by Sunday! See you then. Call whenever you get a chance.

    Yang

I wrote right back:

SUBJECT: RE: CALL & SEX
    Y   ,
Great speaking with you too. Hope you feel better. Regarding your playfulness: It's fun and certainly taken lightly. Don't worry, I'm not getting naked with you either. Not that I'm opposed to getting naked, but I'm not jumping into bed with any man until I feel something amazing. (Like I've never done that before. I've been naked with more men that Wilt Chamberlain… he ain't got nothin' on me!) Look forward to getting to know you and seeing what makes you tick. I don't like to have sex actually, I prefer making love. To build to that takes too long for most guys, as they say they want to get to know someone, but aren't into putting in the time and effort that it takes to build a friendship. So—at this point, I'm looking for a friend. Actually, I've got plenty of friends. But none on the track of having something long-term that could possibly involve naked Twister! LOL

    Be well,
    Y

So the date is set for Sunday, January 22, 2006. I got there late from Brooklyn, fucking A train running on a weekend schedule. Damned Metro fucking workers. Always fixing something when I have to be somewhere. Anyway, I call on my cell to let him know I'm right around the corner. I arrive twelve minutes late according to Sprint time. And he's there. He looks better than his pictures. He's wearing the same coat as in the profile photos. He's granola with a slight crusty hip hop kick to it. Hot? Yes. Good? Yes. He greets me with a kiss. The kiss lands in between the crease of the right side of my lips and my cheek. That's hot already, beginning with the touch. I've already eaten as I don't trust these dates anymore. They are all such a piece of work. Most people don't show up mentally. I hate these dates most of the time, but I put myself out there to ask the universe to send me someone amazing to share my life with.

We sit down. We're in a window seat. The place is slightly empty and quiet. There's light classical music playing in the background. It is cold and sunny. Nice and crisp outside. We begin our barrage of first meeting questions for each other: dating, dates; lovers, loves; things lost, things learned, things gained; and anything that either of us can think of. The time passes. Soon it's two hours later. He's eaten a spinach omelet. He wolfs it down like a real hungry man. Love a man who can eat and isn't afraid of eating food in front of another. I suggest we go for a walk. Actually, I hate walking in the cold, but it gives me more time with him. I've learned that his trip was an hour, so when he goes back to Long Island, he goes back. When we leave Café Rafaella, he guides me through the door first, which opens out onto the street. It's always hot to do that for someone you are interested in. Don't mind receiving or giving that action. It's just a noble thing in my head. As he guides me, he touches the small of my lower back. I get an instant erection. Even being forty, I still get instant erections. I love that. This is going to be a great date, I feel. I begin to get light headed and tingly.

We walk down Seventh Avenue and turn right onto Christopher Street, heading west. There's light traffic along Christopher Street, and we're walking, talking, and not touching. It's cold so the new pier's a little empty, besides the joggers and dog people. We get near the end, just before the funky drapery where there are tables. There are stairs there. I show him New Jersey, places that I've been and where some of my friends live. When I maneuver myself in front of him he encircles me with his arms. Now both of us are facing New Jersey. He is on the top stair of three. I am on stair two. We are equal in height, but now because of the stairs we are obviously not equal. There's a breeze. His coat is open, he has a hat on. The cold does not affect him as much as it does me. I can feel his heart beat. I have the urge to kiss him. I turn around, face him, stand on my tippy toes, and lightly kiss him. Then the real test—I give him a real kiss. No tongue, but the kiss that says, to me at this moment you are amazing. I am thankful that you are here, that I am here, and that the universe allows us this moment in time. He says, "Wow!" He kisses me back amazingly. He grabs my face to bring our faces close together. This is so on, I could rip his clothes off right now, but then I remember the earlier e-mails mentioning that we're not in this for the sex. Right now I feel like saying FUCK THAT!

As we meander back to Christopher Street, he suggests that we go see the eagle in Central Park. Supposedly, it lives in one of the famous buildings near the park. We take the 1 train uptown and claim a two-seater. He's touching me and talking up a storm. Actually, we're both talking up a storm, sort of like old friends catching up. He's rubbing my hand in his, all around it. Again, I get an erection. This time I am ready, it's in a good place and I don't have to move around or jiggle it to get comfortable. I think this guy is causing me to have hot flashes. He so flippin' rocks. He also has this smell that excites me. Sort of foresty, of working outside a lot. I am becoming intoxicated.

He laughs at himself and begins to laugh with me and at me, too. I like that. He has an ease that I'm not used to but that I've wanted in my life for quite some time. He's hot, that's all there is to it. People are looking at us being lovey dovey. I like that, and think: you straight people—this is what you put in my face every-day and I can have this too!

We finally make it to Central Park, still holding hands as we get off the train. He ushers me through the turnstiles with his hand on my lower back again. I swear I can feel the warmth of his hand through my coat, sweater, and two layers of T-shirts. Up on the street, a straight couple asks for directions. The guy looks at our hands. I notice that and lightly squeeze Yang's hand. I think Yang noticed too, he squeezes back and lightly taps the back of my hand against his thigh for the guy to really get an eyeful. I break into a huge smile.

We walk past Tavern on the Green, up to where the lake is. There's a little boat house there. There's also another couple there, a straight couple. They're kissing. We kiss, too. I'm leaning against one of the poles that hold the boat house up. The sky is clear still, there are birds in the water. He tells me what kind they are, a few words about their habitat, what they do, and how they live. I reach for his hand, lightly move him back to the pole, and with such gentleness stick my tongue down his throat. I make love to his mouth right then and there. I give it all I can. The straight couple is totally into me kissing Yang, my guy for the moment. This kiss could win the MTV Movie Award for Best Onscreen Kiss. I want more of him. Only time will tell. We retrace our path back toward Columbus Circle.

On our way we get to this mound of rock off of our original path. Again, he tells me what it is. He looks around for something in the sky. He's holding my right hand in his left, puts his right hand to his face, and makes this loud noise. A few people look in our direction. He keeps making the noise. He keeps holding my hand. Finally, I get what the hell he is doing. He's calling the ea-gle. I get another erection. I am blushing with excitement. I have a huge smile across my face. I want to take him right there on the rock. But why end this wonderful date by getting arrested? The eagle does not call back, but he is not disappointed. Neither am

I, at least by what's happened thus far. I am wet now. I look down, grateful I wore jeans and not the khaki pants that I was going to; I'd have soaked them by now. I'm a huge leaker when I am excited. He looks at me, takes both hands, grabs my face, and kisses me. I could see this man again. OH YEAH! The eagle is calling back, but not the eagle that you are thinking. LOL

As we're leaving the park, he suggests that we go dancing later that night. It's four-ish. He wants to go dancing around eight. That's four hours that he doesn't have a place to go. I suggest that he come to my place, in Brooklyn, but with one rule: no pants can come off. We can make out, shirts off, use our hands, but pants cannot come off. Not this time.

We get on the A train. It's an express and we get a three-seater this time. He is still all up in my hand. I love that. I am a little tired. Thank God I have food at home. It will be a breeze cooking up something for my man. What the hell did I just think? I just met this guy and already he's "my man"? That always seemed odd to me how that changes. When did he become mine? How can he be mine? We walk through Caribbean land/Eastern Prospect Heights and get to my little one bedroom. He thinks it's cute and nicely decorated. I make him my usual dinner for the week: pesto, ziti pasta, Italian sweet sausage with chopped garlic. He wolfs it down and we talk more about love and life and family. I'm on the floor, stretching. I often go there as it calms me down and makes me comfortable. He joins me, asks me to give him some stretching pointers. I help him out and of course we begin to lip lock like at the park just after he had called my eagle. We are rolling around in my Ikea-furnished apartment, on my Ikea rug. We're feeling each other, not below the belt though. But our legs are able to feel each other's cocks. I ask if he wants to go to the bedroom, only five feet away. He agrees, stops me from getting on the bed, kisses the back of my neck. I moan. He takes off my shirt. I'm getting chills all over my body. He's dry humping my backside, my best feature, my ass. I turn, kiss him back, rip his shirts off over his head, almost really tearing them to shreds and throw him on the full-sized bed.

We're a mess of lips, hands, and covered hips, bumping, grinding, being one on the other, other on the one, elbows, arms, forearms, fingers, licking, sucking, touching. We're making love, and my fucking pants are on! SHIT! To hell with the fucking rules!

But, alas, we keep to them, we settle down. Nobody comes. We're okay. We ease off each other. I hold him in my arms. I feel his warmth, breath, skin, hair, and life. He's home, I feel, or I'm home. I feel content. But he says that we have to go soon. He doesn't want to be late for his DJ friend. We get dressed. He tries to fix his hair, eventually applying water to spruce it up. His winter hat messes it all up anyway.

We take the A train to the F train to get to Urge. It's early. It's Sunday and he has to leave soon, and me, too, I'm an early-to-bedder! We bump and grind, as if I haven't had an erection most of the day anyway. We kiss on the dance floor. We have space. He's not that great of a dancer, but definitely hot! Sort of moves interestingly weirdly like. But he definitely has his own groove and rhythm. We even danced on a pole in the bar; the music was good and we were just having fun and he noticed the pole. It was hot.

We take the F train to Penn Station. There's a hockey game getting out. Straight central. Manly men and their bitches! Full out breeder central. He kisses me long and lovingly and then just walks with them to get on the train, like he's said good-bye to his wife, just like they do. But I don't have a vagina and don't want one, though I am glad they exist in the world. God bless all the innies and outies, I always say.

The day after our date, I sent this:

> I have nothing to say but—what the holy fuck was that? I feel like I was blown over by a storm. I was talking with a building mate last night and she laughed at me 'cause I was trying to describe you and I was totally speechless. All I could say was "And he . . ." then silence and then a huge smile—repeatedly. I look forward to any excursion with you. I'm glad no boundaries were crossed too. Thanks for being a complete gentleman.

;-) But we have to talk about those lips of yours. I may need less of them next time, 'cause right now, they're missed! LOL. Let's just say, holding you is all the loving I need right now. If that need changes, I'll discuss it with you. Point: when we were lying in bed, toward the end and you were in my arms, then—I was dancing. To me that was the high point amongst many smaller ones. At that point you just fit. That's the best way I can explain it.

Yeah—I just got myself excited again! LOL

I would love a tour of LI. I've only been to the Ikea and Fire Island. Maybe next time, dancing on the Island? It's dead now, but that leaves more space for us. Any chance of a bar with a pole there? LOL I didn't get the picture you sent last night as I don't have a picture phone. Send the pix(s) to xxxxxxxxxxxx@hotmail.com. Let's communicate that way. Actually not into the Match.com site. Be well my friend, you are in my thoughts,

My best thoughts, all day,

Yin

· · · · ·

EVEN THOUGH WE haven't yet made plans to get together again, and even if I never take the train with all those breeders from Penn Station out to Montauk, this date will always be one of the most memorable experiences of my life.

KINDRED SOULS

VIC BACH

IT WAS THE start of an intense, long-term relationship, the start of love. Of course, neither Will nor I had any way of knowing it.

We first met, awkwardly, in the nether regions of cyberspace. I had placed a personal ad in the *Blade*, headlined Seeking Kindred Soul. (That's how earnest I am, despite my age and advanced education.) I was facing my sixties alone, yet fairly new to gay life. After a few episodic encounters, I was still seeking the male soul mate of my fantasies.

Will lived and worked in Belfast, in telecommunications, but yearned to experience New York. At the age of twenty-five, he followed his impulse and booked an August flight and a two-week stay at a hostel he found on the Internet, in the Chelsea area—four to a room—at a price he could afford. His first e-mail struck a valiant chord: "nothing ventured, nothing gained." My ad interested him, particularly the promise of "good conversation, so lacking in gay life." He wondered if we might meet when he was in the city.

Just eighteen months before, I had moved into my own apartment—a rent-stabilized studio on West 77th Street opposite the American Museum of Natural History—to live separately from my wife. The reasons were complicated and had little to do with sexual leanings or my long-deferred desire for male intimacy. After the move, I felt the aloneness and resolved to come close to another man for once in my life. The late shift in sexual identity was difficult, fumbling, closeted, but it was accomplished. I joined several groups at the Gay, Lesbian, Bisexual, and Transgender Community Center. My few sexual encounters were physically fulfilling but emotionally bankrupt. The longest was three months of "going steady" with a fifty-year-old Brooklyn guy with whom I couldn't hold a decent conversation. When we parted I decided, for the first time, to place an ad in the *Blade*.

One by one I met with the more interesting respondents, and came up dry after a month of screening. Then I received an e-mail response all the way from Ireland, from an articulate young man named William. I was puzzled and surprised; the power of telecommunication was new to me. The idea of meeting him struck me as absurd, given our vast differences in age and culture, and his transient stay in New York. Without answering, I filed the response away with the others in my locked office cabinet.

A week later, responses had dwindled to zero and I decided to shred the file. When I came upon William's note again, on sheer impulse I sent a short message back with my phone number, suggesting he call when he was in the city—we might meet for coffee or a drink. *Why not?* It might be an interesting, if brief intercultural experience. I thought that would end it, but the note began a seductive, six-week correspondence of mounting intensity. We traded photos and several trans-Atlantic phone calls, and planned to meet on August first, the day he arrived.

Given the ocean that parted Will and me, and our differences in age and background, we were not likely candidates to meet offline, even during his visit to the city. That summer of 2000 Manhattan was flush with post-millennial excitement. Tourists flooded the streets, hotels were booked solid, restaurants were more than their usual crowded and noisy. We might have met by chance, I suppose, in a bar, maybe in the park, if I had the nerve for that kind of encounter. But unlikely.

It was Tuesday, August first. I made sure I was home in time to receive Will's call in the early evening when he arrived at the hostel. All week, I had labored to clean the apartment, clearing the layer of dust, scrubbing floors. Some last-minute tidying needed to be done. Then I folded the open futon into a respectable sofa and stowed the bedding in the closet. After I showered, with the phone nearby, I chose my black slacks because they had a slimming effect. The weather was torrid—in the 90s, heavy with humidity. There would be no concealing jacket. Instead, I wore a cool purple, pinstriped shirt, sleeves rolled to mid-arm, and carried a black shirt over my shoulder in case of rain. I was conscious of the care I was taking for a casual meeting that would go nowhere, with a young man who struck me as mousy in his e-mail photo. Despite the ambivalence and the dread, something excited me. It was, after all, a date.

Will's call came later than expected; he, too, had showered and changed. The subway ride down was quick, and I had only a short walk south on Eighth Avenue to the hostel. At West 30th Street, I could see a young man leaning against the brick façade, waiting expectantly. He was boyish-looking, medium height and frame, with blond-brown hair reflecting the evening sun. I called "Will?" and he beamed at me. He had a pleasing, clean-shaven face; his smile was bright and open. The e-mail photo did him no justice. He seemed happy to see me—there was no sign of disappointment.

As we shook hands I pressed my other hand warmly on his shoulder. "Well, at last we meet."

He smiled back. "Amazing, isn't it?"

I hailed a cab on the avenue. Once we were settled inside, I kicked off the conversation.

"Sorry about the traffic, and the weather is unbearable. You're not seeing the city at its best."

"Oh, no, it's wonderful to be here!" His enthusiasm almost shouted. "And so good to meet you in person." He looked away, out the window, and lowered his voice. "I have to admit I'm nervous to the point of shaking." He smiled as if to reassure himself and turned back to me. Our hands found each other and locked below the sight line of the East Indian driver. "I can't tell you how much better it feels to hold your hand," he said. I could feel a slight trembling.

"Yes, it does." I smiled warmly at him, but my critical faculties were active. Despite his pleasant, beaming face and boyish mien, Will was not classically handsome. His teeth had irregularities. He wore thick black eyeglasses—in his photo they made his eyes sag like a beagle's. The fresh-from-the-gym outfit was problematic—his jersey over shirt sported a large embossed star; his trendy three-quarter casual slacks teemed with velcro. He wore a thick silver chain around his neck and clunky sandals on his feet. But the gestalt somehow appealed to me. It was an evening that would pass pleasantly. And our hands had struck an immediate rapport, the fingers folding naturally into one another.

As we inched through the traffic, I pointed out the sights—the theater district, Columbus Circle (his first glimpse of Central Park), and Lincoln Center. At the Greek restaurant I had picked, we took a table at the window, with a good view of Columbus Avenue.

"Thanks for showing me around."

"My pleasure. Do you know where we are?"

"Generally. It's the Upper West Side, isn't it?"

"Yes. And Columbus Avenue is one of its spines."

"I remember now. I've scoured every Web site I could find about the city."

We ordered too much, including red wine. Neither of us has ever been able to remember what we talked about that first night, except for a few fragments. We picked at the food, but the conversation was animated.

"So, is the city living up to your expectations?"

"It's fantastic, even just this taste of it."

"After all our e-mails, I'm still not sure what interested you in coming here? Did you say it was the movie *Hair*?"

"No, that's how I got interested in Central Park. That was later. The reason is so tacky, please don't laugh." I raised my eyebrows in anticipation. "My earliest memories of the city are *Cagney and*

Lacey, . . . on TV? That's when the seed was planted, back in the mid eighties. I loved that show. Then, as a teenager, I saw *An Affair to Remember*. That clinched it."

"The fateful date at the Empire State Building? What a symbol of romantic destiny."

"Yes," he laughed, "I never thought of that."

"You must be a romantic, Will," I teased.

"You've no idea. I still cry whenever I see the movie. I've got the video, seen it a dozen times."

Will's tastes ran to the big releases—he was impatient for the *Harry Potter* and *The Lord of the Rings* epics—and he followed industry news on the Internet.

"How do *your* tastes in film run?" he wanted to know.

"It varies. But I grew up with *film noir*. That's the way I measure reality. Are you familiar with it?"

"Oh, yes—*The Maltese Falcon*, some of the other classics. But I still have a lot of catching up. But they're hard to find in Ireland. The video rental shops shelve only the new films."

"That's too bad. The shops here are a virtual library."

During dinner Will pulled a small gift-wrapped package out of his pack and insisted I open it. It was a book, a recent Gide biography, one my son had also given me for my last birthday. On the inside cover there was an inscription: *A little something so you never forget. Will 2000.*

I had mentioned Gide in my correspondence—I was shocked that so few younger gays knew of him. I was touched at his trying to please me. It took me a moment to regain my balance.

"Thank you . . . You know how important Gide was to gays in my generation?"

"Not really."

"Well, *The Immoralist* was the Rosetta Stone for the closeted. And Gide's diaries were mind-blowing. But I'm waxing on . . ."

When the time came to leave, most of dinner was still on the table. Will insisted on treating; "I really appreciate your taking the time."

Despite the muggy weather and the threat of rain, we agreed to walk to my apartment. We strolled up West 72nd Street past the Dakota, as I'd planned. Will recognized the entryway where Lennon was killed. As we walked, he lit a cigarette, assuring me he wouldn't smoke in the apartment. On Central Park West, the park stretched out before us. I thought we might enter it—I had planned to dart in and offer Will a first kiss. Our correspondence had nourished that affection; his boyish, warm presence sharpened the impulse. But the park was overrun with people scurrying to a scheduled concert on the Great Lawn.

We reached my building and casually walked past the concierge, who was engrossed in some Spanish-language television show. Once the elevator door shut, Will and I were alone for the first time. From his corner of the elevator, Will smiled at me, a smile that radiated affection and expectation. I recall the moment—it also radiated an inkling of devotion, a spark that emboldened me, freed me to do as I pleased. I moved toward him, pressed him gently to the wall, and kissed him, finally. His lips and tongue were supple and responsive.

"You are cheeky," he joked, when the elevator stopped at my floor.

"We've waited for this moment for six weeks. Hardly a bold move."

Inside the apartment, I took him to the window and showed him the view of the museum. It had become my standard opening stratagem. He took it in as I approached him from behind. Before I even touched him, he quickly turned back to me and placed his body firmly against mine, craning his face forward for another kiss. It evolved into a thorough embrace. Our dance proceeded. I poured us wine and we spoke; our conversation, easy and rambling, alternated with embraces that ratcheted up in intensity. The six-week correspondence, the phone conversations, added a familiarity, a sense of closeness to the attraction I felt.

The signals were clear. While Will washed up, I unfolded and made up the futon. I quickly hid the Gide biography my son had given me, so Will wouldn't notice his was a duplicate. He emerged from the bathroom in snug boxer shorts; he was lovely, a faun-like creature with a light carpeting of auburn hair. He had a gently muscled torso, defined but soft to the touch. He helped me off with my clothes. When at last he lowered his shorts I saw he was uncircumcised, his penis was large and semi-hard.

In memory, our first lovemaking was not remarkable. But, from the start, we shared a sensual vocabulary. Based in affection, our lovemaking mounted to a crescendo of sensation, stirred by intense caresses, the wandering of lips and tongues across each other's bodies, and frequent returns "home"—face-to-face—for needed kisses. We coped with the condoms, then each of us focused on the other's genitals. Once we had brought each other to ejaculation, we lay in each other's arms.

"Do you know how beautiful you are?" he asked. He stroked my side.

"No. I don't think of myself that way." I recalled the painful glimpses of my sagging body at moments I came upon myself in the mirror.

"No, I bet you don't."

"And I'm ancient."

"No, you're just right, more than that. You know I don't fancy younger men."

"You're the lovely one, Will. But those tattoos on your arms—how can you do that to yourself?" He had an inch-wide Celtic pattern ringing each of his upper arms. They reminded me of his silver choker.

"Don't you like them? I love them. They're very popular, you know."

We lay there for a while, our hands exploring each other. Will seemed exhausted and fell asleep quickly. I realized he must be jet-lagged. There was no question we would spend the night together. It was never discussed.

The alarm woke us in the morning. No time for lingering, I had to get to work. Will ran into the kitchen when he heard the whirr of the coffee grinder. Like me, he was addicted to coffee, but he was new to the ritual. We had a pleasant breakfast and cleaned up. Will took in the view in the morning sun. We showered together and left the apartment at the same time. He needed careful instructions for the subway back to the hostel, and then up to Times Square, one of his prime tourist destinations. We made no specific plans, but agreed to stay in touch by phone and meet in the evening at the apartment. I didn't give him the keys, nor did he ask for them. It went unsaid that he wasn't to use the apartment while I was out.

What did I feel that morning as we parted on the subway? I was exuberant, if a bit tired. It had gone well, at least as it had been planned, without awkwardness, hurt, or second thoughts. I had carried it off with my young friend and that felt good. Nothing more needed to be done or worried through, other than handling whatever came up today.

By late morning Will called me at the office. He had run into two Irish girls staying at the hostel. They invited him to join them that evening at a local tavern that featured Irish dancing. He sounded enthusiastic. I refrained from asking if I could join; I was aware of the age difference and not about to impose myself. He would call from the tavern to let me know his plans. Once I hung up the phone, I realized I had no idea whether I would ever see Will again.

It was ten-thirty in the evening and I hadn't heard from Will. He had decided to go on to better things. We had our encounter, now there were others to be had. The Irish girls were a convenient excuse, maybe a construction. Somber as my disappointment was, I felt a sense of relief. I couldn't deny some lingering anxiety about having another tryst. At least I wouldn't be required to perform again. Men of a certain age—many of them—struggle with uncertainties about sexual performance, even at the crest of excitement. I was no exception. The prospect of failing with a male partner was even more daunting; you could trust women to be more accepting. Another evening with Will might find me—

how to put it?—less responsive. If he didn't call, I wouldn't be put to the test.

Suddenly the phone rang. It was Will. "I've been thinking—what on earth am I doing here? With the girls? I really want to be with you. I'm on my way, sweet—if that's okay with you. It should take me, what, about ten minutes?"

I was stoic. "Stay as long as you like. Just ring up from the lobby whenever you get here."

"No, no, I'm coming right now."

I was pleased. Our quirky relationship was still in play. But I waxed nervous about what to do with him, whether I was up to it. It occurred to me that I should take the initiative. I ought to concentrate on working at him. That might be the best way to distract from any problems I might have.

When Will arrived we had some wine, this time on an already open futon. He was energized about his day in the city. We talked like old friends, long parted, happy to see each other. Again, the conversation became an affectionate seduction—we kissed and caressed as we spoke. He was delighted when I began to undress him.

I held him aside while I arranged several pillows against the wall on the far side of the bed. By now he was naked. He smiled at me—again that radiant trust—while I seated him, his back against the pillows, his legs folded out toward me. He was puzzled, but curious, expectant about what I had in mind.

I took off the rest of my clothes and approached him. Kneeling in the space between his legs, I faced him and moved my body close to his. I started at his lips, with several long, penetrating kisses that he returned in kind. Then, with my tongue, I slowly circumnavigated his face and head. It dwelled on his cheeks, lapped at his ears, slid across his forehead. Then it discovered the soft tissue above and below his eyes, and every contour of his neck and under jaw. I comprehended each of his features with my tongue and lips, returning frequently to his mouth for lingering kisses. Very soon he purred with pleasure. I was struck by his openness to being loved so.

I moved to his chest, and to each of his nipples, where he was exquisitely sensitive. Then to his underarms, the most erogenous of zones, where the lapping at his armpits unnerved him and his purrs turned to agonized murmurs. His sizeable erection grew firmer. Since he wasn't wearing a condom, I noticed for the first time that erect dicks look alike, circumcised or not. He trembled with pleasure and drew my face to his, kissing me passionately, as if to halt my progress and give his sensations pause. I continued my journey at his arms, and slowly slid my way past the tattoos, along the sinuous contours of his muscles to his hands and fingers, each of which I took into my mouth in turn, and thoroughly bathed.

Then I returned to his lower chest below the breasts. My tongue conscientiously traced the outline of each rib as it arced upward from the central sternum. Will groaned with intense, nearly unbearable pleasure. At the same time his hands were mobile; he lightly caressed my wandering head, or moved down to cradle and knead my testicles or stroke my cock. It was intoxicating to pleasure Will in this way, and ask for little or nothing back, other than his purring acknowledgment. I was growing confident of my power to excite Will and gaining some confidence in myself. I was eager to move on—his body was a continent I had only just begun to explore.

When I was done, we turned to each other and kissed deeply. He heaved a long sigh of satisfaction. I could feel his pulsing erection at my groin.

"No one has ever done that to me before," he whispered. He seemed puzzled at the gap in his experience. As he lay in my arms, smiling at me, he was overcome with sensation, still in an excited state, vibrating with pleasure. I was surprised he could control orgasm for that long.

"I've never done it to anyone before. Someone once did a little of it to me."

"You are so hot . . ."

"Whatever that means." Could "hot" correlate with perfor-mance anxiety? "Well, it's my gift to you—so you never forget." I lowered my body to go down on him.

"No, now I want to do it to you."

I demurred. "Tomorrow, sweet. It's late."

But he insisted, and I submitted. Will did very well at the model I had only just innovated. He had a talent for reciprocity. I responded in kind. The sensations came in waves, from sheer sensate pleasure to intervals beyond any control. Through it I sus-tained a firm erection. When he was done with me, we were both full of each other and spent with pleasure, yet neither of us had come. To consummate, we masturbated each other as we kissed using K-Y jelly for lubricant—we had no use for condoms at this point. Will exploded quickly, in a forceful and abundant stream. I came soon after.

I was so taken by Will, by his young beauty, so ecstatic about our physical communion, even more by the affectionate bond, that I pressed close to him as we kissed, near to the point of crushing each other. Will pulled his face away for a moment and stroked my chest.

"There's something I've got to tell you, Vic."

"What?"

"I've always wanted someone who comes close and kisses once we've come, who understands how important that moment is."

"Doesn't everyone?"

"No. Most men I've known have their squirt, say thank you, and turn over."

I was moved. "Not us. No, not us." We moved together again, kissed tenderly for a while, and fell asleep, our semen-soaked bod-ies folded together.

The next morning I awoke before the alarm. I lay there for several minutes gazing at Will as he slept, his face inches from mine. He was so trusting and innocent as he lay there, his head on my shoulder. I had not known any man so beautiful, or so well. When it was time I moved forward and kissed him gently on the lips to wake him. In his sleep, his lips opened and admitted me, responding fully to the thrusts of my tongue, and we embraced closely. In our years together, I cannot remember Will not being ready for or open to my affection. Or I to his.

BIRTHDAYS &
ANNIVERSARIES

WILL YOU STILL FEED ME?

TOM MENDICINO

MIDDLE AGE HAD advanced by stealth, allowing me to sail through my thirties blissfully unaware of its relentless assault. It seemed like I awoke one morning and, overnight, I'd progressed beyond "thinning" to "balding," that my twenty-nine-inch waist had expanded to thirty-three (on an empty stomach), and that my naked eye needed assistance to decipher road signs and distinguish the shadows flickering across the television screen. Suddenly, I was approaching the milestone that once had loomed so far in the distant future that it had been as inconceivable as sprouting wings. I was counting the months, then the weeks, and, finally, the days until I turned forty.

There wasn't a rational explanation for this unexpected obsession with the calendar. I'm not a narcissist according to the criteria of the *Diagnostic and Statistical Manual of Mental Disorder*. And while I don't have a face to make a baby cry or a dog howl, I'd never possessed the degree of physical beauty that would justify self-indulgent mourning for the passing of youth. But there I was, reduced to a pathetic cliché. Reasoned analysis (*It's better than the alternative*) and greeting card sentiments (*You're not getting older, you're getting better*) were useless. Ignoring the inevitable (*It's just another day*) was impossible.

My shrink said we needed to talk about it, girding for battle by kicking off her Birkenstocks and folding her legs. But as I droned on, she leaned forward in her chair, peering at her busy fingers, more interested in rolling a cigarette than in the hackneyed whin-

ing of a no-longer young male homosexual approaching a land-
mark birthday. She reminded me that it might be understandable
that a woman, racing against her biological clock, might sink into
depression on the eve of her fifth decade. A man of that age, however, is just beginning to reap the fruits of his labor as his hard
work and perseverance begin to pay off and he enters the decades
of his greatest influence and power.

"I suppose so," I said, punctuating my reluctant concession
with a deep sigh.

"You know Tom, you're right. You are getting old," she said,
playing with the god-awful dangling earrings she'd probably
bought at a lesbian craft show. "I'll try to have the office wheel-
chair accessible before your appointment next week." She cut
loose with a rumbling Bea Arthur cackle that made me want to
start singing "Thank You for Being a Friend".

My partner, Nick, who'd graduated to middle age eight years
earlier, tried to be patient, alternating between reassuring ("You
don't look a day over thirty . . . maybe thirty-six") to exasperated
("Jesus Christ, will you just shut up about it"). A physician who'd
been treating the community since the beginning of the epidemic,
he'd turned forty in the darkest days of the crisis, before the development of drug therapies that eventually downgraded the disease
from fatal to chronic. Gay men didn't complain about birthdays
in the mid-eighties. A decade later, medical advances had made it
possible to again be self-indulgent and mildly ridiculous about the
aging process.

"So what do you want for your birthday?" he asked a week
before the big day.

"Nothing."

"All right."

"You don't have to be so agreeable," I grumbled.

"Then tell me what it is you want."

"To pretend it's not happening."

"All right."

"I'm serious!" I protested, hoping the tone of my voice would inspire a surprise party. A trip to Europe wouldn't be unwelcome either.

"Okay, I believe you," he said.

The invitations were probably already in the mail and the tickets charged to American Express.

"I'd be happy with a meat loaf," I said, as if my primary concern was that my birthday wish would be considerate of his wallet and not impose any extraordinary demands on his time.

"I think I can do that," he said, as if I might believe he would commemorate such an important event with something as mundane as a meat loaf.

I started practicing my surprised expression in the mirror.

. . . . .

I WAS BORN at 11:00 A.M. on Mother's Day, and as fate would have it, my fortieth birthday again fell on this holiday. But if I was looking for sympathy, it wasn't coming from dear sweet Mom.

"How do you think *I* feel being the mother of a middle-aged man?" she asked. "So how are you going to spend your special day?"

I paused, suspecting a trick question. I couldn't tell her Nick was throwing me a surprise party because her feelings would be hurt if she hadn't been invited. Unless, of course, the birthday call was a setup. Not being in the vanguard of telecommunications advances like caller-ID, I'd assumed, probably mistakenly, that she was calling from her home in Pittsburgh instead of a room at the Sheraton Society Hill four blocks away, where she was holed up until party time.

"Well I hope the weather's as gorgeous in Philly as it is here," she said. Nice try, I thought as I thanked her for the card and the check and hung up.

"Why don't you take your bike out this afternoon?" Nick suggested. He'd started the day with a bad joke, wishing me a happy birthday and asking if I felt as old as I looked. He seemed antsy as I dawdled, and as I was leaving he asked what time I expected to be back. I told him I thought I'd bike down to the stadium and maybe go to the gym afterward. I waited for him to ask if I could make it a little earlier or, perhaps, a little later.

"Okay," he said as I pedaled away.

It was going to take a superhuman effort to get the house ready for the guests that were expected in a few short hours. He must have sweet-talked (and was overpaying) Carol the cleaning lady to do a Sunday afternoon kamikaze sweep through the public rooms. I was so preoccupied with deciphering possible clues that a taxi racing to beat a red light almost ensured that my fortieth birthday would be my last. I slammed the brake, flipped the bird to the passing cab, and decided to change my route to quieter, and presumably safer, side streets. Three miles later, I'd solved the mystery! I would arrive home and Nick would tell me to put on a collared shirt because someone—Chris and Harry, Laura maybe—had called with a spontaneous dinner invitation. He'd accepted without bothering to consult me because *it is your birthday and we ought to do SOMETHING*. Having practiced my reaction, I would appear genuinely astonished when thirty or forty of my nearest and dearest friends jumped from their hiding places behind the furniture and shouted happy birthday!

I was only mildly disappointed when I slipped my key in the lock and was greeted at the front door by deafening silence. But if the celebrants were gathering at that very moment at Chris and Harry's, or maybe Laura's, why were cooking smells coming from the kitchen? While I was gone, Nick had gone all out: linen napkins, good china, tulips and daisies, candles. He'd set a beautiful table. For two.

"Happy birthday, Mendo," he said, not looking away from the pot he was stirring. Damn, it was hard to be mad when he was at his most vulnerable, squinting to read Marcella Hazen's small print while a bead of sweat dangled from his nose, threatening to drip into the marinara. The kitchen definitely did not smell vegetarian.

"Meatballs?" I asked.

"Close."

"Huh?"

"One big meatball," he said, pulling the pan from the oven. "You said you wanted meat loaf."

A Prussian by birth and temperament, he'd fallen in love with all things Italian, including me and the cuisine of my heritage. He was happily drizzling balsamic over greens and toasted pine nuts. Onions were braising on the stovetop. He poured me a glass of wine and banished me from the kitchen. I wandered into the living room and flopped on the sofa. The disc player was loaded with Sinatra in the Columbia and Capital years; Old Blue Eyes crooning *One for My Baby* wasn't helping my mood. This birthday was turning out to be one more in the long string of uneventful milestones. I hadn't had a memorable celebration since the trip to the drive-in when I turned ten, fighting with a carload of boys while my father's eyes glazed over at Vincent Price camping it up in a cheap American International movie inspired by Edgar Allan Poe. The only thing I could recall about my twentieth was falling into a boxwood hedge, courtesy of an encounter with Jack Daniel's. I was stranded in a motel room in Albany as I turned thirty, staying up until three to watch a John Carpenter festival on HBO. A meat loaf and a slice of cake didn't seem to be the type of celebration that was likely to be enhanced by nostalgia in the years to come. At least Sinatra was serenading us with something a bit more cheery as we sat down to eat.

"Happy birthday, Mendo," Nick said again, raising his glass. "I'm glad you didn't want a party. I was hoping tonight would just be the two of us."

When you've lived together for years, it's easy to forget that it's not just anyone who you can wake up with each morning and fall asleep next to each night. Familiarity may not breed contempt but complacency certainly can cause you to take your happiness for granted. Bitching about this and moaning about that, you overlook that the life you've come to regard as mundane and ordinary is actually something rare and precious. Sometimes it takes the crisis of middle age and the gift of a meat loaf for you to realize that you are a fortunate man indeed to have found someone who loves you back with the same intensity with which you love him.

I could have told him how much he meant to me, how happy I was, that I intended to spend the rest of my life with him. But he's shy and declarations make him uncomfortable. So instead I asked about the doorstop-thick tome on World War I he'd been reading, inviting a history lesson that began with the assassination in Sarajevo and continued through the impact of the *Dreadnought* on the military outcome. His voice has a musical cadence, low with the hint of a childhood stutter. He has a gift for spinning facts into story that would be the envy of any college lecturer. His curiosity and mental agility have never ceased to amaze me, and at forty, I had many years ahead to learn from him. An hour later, after signing the Treaty of Versailles and adding a short postscript on the fate of the Hapsburgs, he cleared the table, usually my job, returning with a chocolate cake from Rindelaub's Bakery, four candles blazing.

"Make a wish."

I nodded and sat back and folded my arms when he expected me to lean forward and blow out the candles.

"Did you make a wish?"

"Yes."

"Then blow out the candles."

"I can't."

"Why not? Hurry up, the wax is dripping on the cake."

"You didn't sing 'Happy Birthday'."

"Don't hold your breath. Blow out the candles."

"Not until I get my wish."

"What's your wish?"

"That you sing 'Happy Birthday'."

We'd been together for over fifteen years and I'd never heard him so much as hum or whistle, let alone sing. He was convinced he couldn't carry a tune. He swore no mortal had ever been cursed with such a wretched vocal instrument. He was, of course, the complete opposite of me. I exercised my lungs on a daily basis at a volume that would have made a banshee blush.

"Come on. You wouldn't want to deprive me of one teensy-weensy wish!"

The candles were quickly burning down to nubs.

"How many times am I going to turn forty?"

"Jesus. All right, all right. *Happybirthdaytoyouhappybirthdayto-youhappybirthdaydearMendohappybirthdaytoyou.*

"Doesn't count."

"Yes, it does."

"No, it doesn't. First, you didn't sing it. You spoke it. Second, you raced through it so fast the words ran together."

"Well that's the best you're going to get."

It was time to pull the ace from my sleeve.

"When did you stop loving me?"

"About five minutes ago, when you started harping about me singing to you. Now blow out the damn candles."

"I'll never ask you again. I promise."

"Oh for God's sake."

"Please."

He swallowed hard, the glitch in his throat betraying his bravado. He was as nervous as if he were being asked to perform for an audience of music critics at Carnegie Hall. But in a small, hesitant and charming voice, he sang 'Happy Birthday' to me.

"Satisfied?"

"Not yet."

"What now?"

"Sing 'When I'm Sixty-Four'."

"Don't push it."

I stood and kissed him on the forehead.

"This will make you happy," he said, uncorking a bottle of Veuve Clicquot. Even an Iron City clod like me knew this bottle was the gold standard. I blew out the candles.

One good toast deserved another, each one sillier than the last as the champagne went to our heads.

To you!

To me!

To chocolate cake!

To meat loaf!

To Pepto-Bismol!

To Maalox!

"I don't think I can eat another bite," I said, loosening my belt. I was a little unsteady on my feet as I rose from the table.

"No chores for you tonight," he said. "I'll load the dishwasher and be up in a minute."

A package and two envelopes were waiting for me on the bed. He'd bought me a broadcloth shirt, pale blue to set off my eyes, and a bold red tie. In one of the envelopes I found two tickets, Phillies versus Pirates, and a card that read *I hope you don't expect me to go with you. Devotion has its limits.*

"I suppose a roll in the hay is out of the question," he said as he flopped next to me on the bed. A burp was my answer.

"I figured," he laughed. "Why don't you check out what's in the video player."

If I had any doubt that he truly, deeply loved me, such misgivings were banished from my mind when I hit the remote and Sissy Spacek started soaping between her legs. My thoughtful, considerate partner had made the sacrifice to subject himself to his four-hundredth viewing of *Carrie* and, for one night, he didn't object as I recited all the lines. He'd really intended to stay awake to keep me company and be an audience for my performance. But he'd worked so hard giving me the perfect birthday I couldn't begrudge him a good night's sleep. I threw a blanket over him and let him snore through the prom.

· · · · ·

WHAT WAS IN the second envelope? A pair of US Airways tickets. We celebrated my belated fortieth birthday eating our way across Europe. I know it was a spectacular adventure, but hard as I try, I can't remember a single one of those meals.

CHRISTMAS IN JULY

MICHAEL G. CORNELIUS

FOR OUR FIRST anniversary Joe picked me up in his sporty blue Chevy, gave me a couple of books I'd been wanting (always a good gift for an English major), bought me lunch at the same Chinese food place where we'd had our first date, took me to a movie, and then walked with me hand-in-hand along the beach as the sun went down. As he drove me home, I thought to myself that we had had a really nice day—until I opened my apartment door and saw Manny there waiting for us. Manny was the waiter for the caterer Joe had hired to surprise me with an intimate, gourmet dinner for two served right in my crummy, cramped apartment. Five sumptuous courses later I was sated, deliriously happy, and more in love than ever—and determined as hell to one-up Joe the next year.

It's not that we're competitive with each other—really, we're not. And I didn't feel as if Joe was expecting me to top what he had done last year. But like so many other gay men, I do have a flair for the dramatic. And I was just so moved and so thrilled with what Joe had surprised me with on our first anniversary that I wanted to give him those same feelings on our second. But there was a catch; I was broke. Actually, I was beyond broke. I was poor. Whereas Joe was gainfully employed as a teacher, I was in the second year of my Ph.D. program in medieval literature, a vocation I adored but which had already left me in serious debt. Thoughts of whisking Joe away for a magical vacation on a remote tropical island gave way to reality as I stared at the boxes of twenty-nine-cent macaroni and cheese and endless packages of Ramen noodles that were the staple of my grad school diet. Whatever I was going to do for him, I'd have to do it on the cheap.

For months I racked my brain, but as the big day loomed, I began to despair. I couldn't think of a thing. Sure, I had picked him up a few gifts I knew he'd like, but a token or two of my love was hardly the equivalent of what he had surprised me with the previous year. And while Joe was certainly not expecting me to do anything huge for our anniversary, I expected it of myself. Feeling the pressure (not to mention the heat of a July summer without air conditioning), I tossed and turned in bed, one small plastic fan barely enough to keep me from passing out in the stifling weather. Finally, exhausted and frustrated beyond words at four in the morning, I drifted off into an uneasy sleep.

I woke surprisingly refreshed, and even more importantly, I woke with an idea. To this day I'm not sure why, but something sparked in my mind a memory of the first Christmas Joe and I had spent together. The little artificial tree that was the highlight of my apartment's decorations was only three feet tall, but as we covered it with shiny gold and silver balls, freshly bought at the local Wal-Mart, I had begun to reminisce about the Norman Rockwell-like Christmases of my childhood in upstate New York. Memory served up wintry affairs with tons of presents piled under the tree and my large and boisterous family itching with anticipation for the big day to come. Joe's family, in contrast, had hardly celebrated the holiday. His parents were working-class immigrants who each worked two jobs and scrimped and saved every penny along the way to afford a nice house and the daily necessities of life for their two sons. Christmas, in their estimation, was a luxury other people could afford, and Joe didn't even receive a Christmas gift from them until he was into his teens. My family, by contrast, though poor ourselves, had always done Christmas to death, our fifteen-foot trees scraping the roof of the cathedral ceiling in our log cabin home while my mother and sisters all baked copious piles of cookies we'd be eating until Easter. As I

CHRISTMAS IN JULY   { 81 }

told story after story of our Cornelius family holidays, Joe always looked both wistful and engrossed, and had often remarked how he wished he had once had a Christmas like that.

So I decided: I was going to give it to him. But not in December—right now, in July. That's how I'd surprise him for our second anniversary—with Christmas in July.

Yawning, I turned over and glanced and my alarm clock. Holy crap! It was already 11:00. Joe was going to come down after he got off work. That meant he'd be here by 5:00. That gave me six hours to turn a blistering hot July day into the Currier and Ives Christmas of Joe's dreams. Bounding out of bed, I pulled the holiday decorations out of the hall closet and began to set them up. Actually, first I had to clean my apartment. Like any grad student, all the tables and chairs of my tiny place were covered with books and papers strewn about in a seemingly random order. It would take too long for me to put everything away in its proper place; besides, technically speaking, everything already *was* in its proper place. At first I contemplated throwing everything onto my bed, but if the evening went as I hoped, Joe and I would end up in the bed ourselves. So rethinking that plan I stuffed everything into my cedar chest, which was actually an old Gateway computer box that stored extra linens and shirts. Shoving books and papers into it, I finally had the room cleared enough to begin decorating.

I began with the tree. True, it was only three feet tall, but I don't have the nimblest of fingers, and even under the best of circumstances putting that little tree together was an arduous chore for me. Now, under a time crunch, I found myself constantly frustrated as I jammed the branches into whatever hole would take them. The tree began to look a little lopsided—at one point I even considered telling Joe that our tree had leprosy to explain its misshapen appearance—but I managed to pull it together. I still had to fluff it up, to make the branches actually resemble a tree instead of a hat stand. Fluffing is not one of my strong suits (no porn jokes, please!) but in the end I managed to get one side of the tree to resemble—well, a tree. The other side I placed firmly against the wall and out of sight.

Out came the trimmings! I strung a set of multicolored lights across the front, but then remembering that Joe preferred white lights, I took them off and put the white ones on instead. Next came the balls, and then the few spare ornaments we'd picked up here and there. A large red ribbon adorned the top. I wasn't particularly fond of it, but it had only cost fifty cents and was the cheapest tree topper I could find. Finally, I put on the garland, a feathered serpent to coil around the top of tree, and stood back to admire my handiwork. Hmm. The tree resembled less Norman Rockwell and more Salvador Dali, but by now it was 1:00 and I still had a lot of ground to cover. It would have to do.

I had already wrapped Joe's presents in some red and yel- low striped paper that screamed more lesbian summer wedding and less Happy Ho-Ho-Ho. I tore the paper off the gifts and rewrapped them, this time in green paper covered with jaunty wreaths and golden bells. I placed the three gifts under the tree. To be honest, they hadn't looked like much before, but now they looked even worse—puny, to be precise, even if the tree only was three feet tall. I decided that I needed to pick up a few more things and get them wrapped if I was really going to make this resemble a true Christmas extravaganza.

Food! I was planning on taking Joe out to the same Chinese restaurant we had gone to on our first date and first anniversary, but a Christmas theme called for dinner at home. I didn't have the time or the skill to cook a turkey. In fact, the only dish I made that Joe would even deign to eat was my pasta Bolognese. Fortunately, he considered it one of his favorite dishes of all time (or so he told me, and I chose to believe him). I hastily checked my freezer. Yes, I had some ground beef I could thaw—but I was missing about half the ingredients from the sauce. And what about salad, bread, hors d'oeuvres, dessert? What about the fricking Christmas cookies? Clearly, a trip to the store was in order.

But this is where I hit another snag. I couldn't actually afford a car payment *and* grad school, and I lived close enough to the university to walk to my classes, so I had long operated under the premise that I had no need for a vehicle. But the closest grocery store was a good seven miles from my house. In fact, the only shops in walking distance were a convenience store and a pharmacy. I felt panic setting in. *You can do this*, I said to myself. *You'll just need to improvise a bit.*

I hadn't showered yet, and I didn't even have time to put any product in my hair before setting out for the store. It was at least ninety degrees outside, with humidity to match, but I jogged over to the two shops, determined to save myself as much time as possible. Luckily, the convenience store had jars of Ragu I could use as the base of the sauce, but no tomato paste to thicken it with. I looked at what they did have. Mashed potato flakes? Parmesan cheese? Barbecue sauce? What the hell. I threw it all in my basket. I scurried into the next aisle. The store carried no produce of any kind save for two bruised apples, one paltry lemon, and a cantaloupe. I left the apples and grabbed the other two. Dessert . . . I had no hope of finding Christmas cookies or anything to make them with. I grabbed a bag of Chips Ahoy and some green and red icing tubes. I also picked up some chocolate sauce, whipped cream, and heavy cream—all the ingredients for a cheap and easy chocolate mousse. It seemed like a viable option for dessert, though I had never actually made a chocolate mousse before. In fact, I had never made any kind of mousse before. If worse came to worse, I reasoned, I could be the dessert, and the whipped cream and chocolate sauce would come in handy then, too.

I ran across to the drug store, frantic as my watch rounded 2:00. The sky had darkened considerably, but I barely noticed as I scoured the aisles to add a few presents to Joe's pile. A joke book went into my basket. Lottery tickets. A journal. A copy of *People* magazine. A water pistol. Some Canada mints, some Ferrero Rocher chocolates, and just for laughs, a box of stool softener. Heck, if dinner turned out as I feared, that might be as handy as the chocolate sauce.

As I left the drug store, the heavens split open and a heavy summer thunderstorm rained down upon me. I half-trotted, half-trudged the half mile back to my apartment, hunching my body over my bags to keep everything from getting soaked and cursing my idiocy for not bringing an umbrella with me. Still, I never wavered. And I never thought for a moment that Joe wasn't worth every bit of drama and trauma in throwing together a last-minute Christmas in July. Still, those fond thoughts didn't entirely keep me from hurling epithets at the sky and wishing I had thought of this grand idea a few days in advance.

When I got home it was nearly 3:00. Drenched, exhausted, and stinky, I still needed to cook dinner, set the table, wrap the new gifts, find a Christmas card somewhere in my stationery drawer, and clean myself up. I thawed the hamburger in the microwave and got out the holly-covered plastic tablecloth that Joe had bought me last Christmas. I had told him that the tablecloth seemed a bit over the top when he bought it, but now I was glad for his prescience. I set the table, then hastily threw all the ingredients I had into the sauce: the Ragu base, some barbecue sauce, the potato flakes and parmesan cheese to thicken the concoction. Digging deep under the sink, I pulled out the only bottle of wine in my entire apartment, a dusty red someone had brought to a party when I had first moved in. I threw some of that in, too, and then a dash of Tabasco for good measure. Though I lacked onions and garlic, I made up for it with onion and garlic powder, as well as healthy dashes of thyme, rosemary, dried parsley, and marjoram. I let the sauce simmer while I wrapped the rest of the presents and put them under the tree. Now it looked better. I went back to my tiny galley kitchen and sampled the sauce. Not bad, but it needed a little something. Peering into my nearly empty fridge, I pulled out a stick of butter and threw about a quarter of it into the pot. Hey, as the saying goes, everything's better with Blue Bonnet on it. For good measure, I added another healthy dollop of the barbecue sauce as well.

I took the cantaloupe and balled it up, heaping the pieces into two small custard dishes. I stuck them in the fridge to cool. Depending on how my mousse came out, I reasoned the cantaloupe could be either salad or dessert. I looked frantically for my blender, ready to whip the cream for the mousse. I looked, and looked, and looked . . . and finally remembered my friend Lynda had borrowed the blender for her margarita party last month and I had never bothered to get it back. I checked my watch. 3:40. Too late now.

I scanned my cupboards frantically and saw a box of instant chocolate pudding. I grabbed the little box. Fortunately, I had just enough milk left in my fridge. Leaving the pudding to set, I finished setting a romantic table for two (the salad forks, water glasses, and non-disposable plates being the obvious difference between a *non*-romantic table for two). Then I came back to the pudding, and mixed half of the whipped cream with it. Hmm. Not bad. I layered the pudding with the remaining whipped cream and crumbled up bits of Chips Ahoy in a large glass parfait bowl, standing back when I was done to survey the results of my work. Honestly, I don't think Martha Stewart could have made it any prettier. I popped the "mousse" in the refrigerator and went on to my next task.

I set water to boil for the pasta and strung the leftover strand of colored lights on the bookshelf near my dining table. I put up the remaining few Christmas trimmings: a wooden train that spelled NOEL despite three missing wheels; a fat and dusty Santa candle that I thought would make a whimsical centerpiece for the table; and a dilapidated, worn-out, dingy plastic snowman I had named Homeless Joe after the guy I was doing all this for. I then popped into my bathroom and showered, shaved, and shat in record time. I put on a generous spritz of Joe's favorite cologne, Obsession for Men, and brushed my teeth and styled my hair at the same time, nearly confusing my hair gel and the tube of Sensodyne toothpaste. I threw on some shorts and a clean striped polo shirt. No Christmas sweaters for me—it was still ninety degrees in my apartment. Joe would have to consider this a Norman Rockwell Christmas in Sudan.

It was almost 4:15. I tossed the pasta into the rapidly boiling water and dug around for some extra candles for ambience.

I sliced up lemon wedges for the water glasses and managed to find two matching wine glasses, which needed to be hastily washed of the thick coat of dust that circumnavigated their rims. I then made a mess of my CD rack looking for the only Christmas music I owned. My mother had received it free with a full tank of gas last December, but hey, it had Julie Andrews singing "Adeste Fidelis," so I knew it couldn't be all bad. I popped it into my stereo and checked the pasta. Still a bit chewy. I ran back and dug out a leftover card from the previous holiday season. Checking the pasta again, I drained it, and combined it with the sauce and a generous handful of shredded Monterey Jack cheese (that was all I had in the house). Shoot! Bread! The convenience store had had nothing but the same sliced bread I had at home, so I took four slices of wheat and slathered them with butter, parmesan cheese, garlic powder, onion powder, and rosemary. Popping them into the oven, I looked again at the cantaloupe and grabbed a jar of strawberry jelly from the fridge. I scooped a few tablespoons into a dish and zapped it in the microwave for twenty seconds, then spread the thinned sauce all over the melon. I gave it a taste. Not bad.

It was 4:30. I still had to write out the card, make some reasonable facsimile of Christmas cookies, finish the garlic bread, put together a—What was that? The crunch of gravel in the driveway alerted me that someone was coming. I looked out the window. It was Joe! He was early. Joe was never early! Why was Joe early? Of course—since it was our anniversary, he'd probably left work a little early to spend a little more time with me. I sighed. Wasn't that fricking nice of him? Cursing some more under my breath, I hastily scrawled a one-sentence message on the card and slid it under his plate. I turned off the oven and pulled out the bread. Abandoning all other ideas, I grabbed my book bag and my keys and slipped quietly out of my apartment and down the back stairs.

You see, to really one-up Joe, I knew I had to make this a big surprise, and I thought it would be clever (if not a tad cruel) of me to have Joe believe we had both coincidentally arrived at my apartment at the same time. That way, when I opened the door, he'd really be in for a surprise. Fortunately, the driveway was in the back of the building, so I had enough time to sneak down the side stairs and around the corner to the front of my building to meet Joe just as he was heading up the stairs, a small bag of anniversary gifts in his hands.

"Hi, honey!" he said, clearly surprised to see me. I gave him a quick glance (I had to; he's just so damned handsome!) before launching into my role of the aggrieved boyfriend who'd just had the day from hell. I hunched my shoulders and trudged up to him slowly. Looking up to see him I managed to squeeze out a few tears. I've always been able to cry on cue; it was a useful skill as a child negotiating days off of school with my mother and is still handy in numerous awkward social situations.

"What's wrong?" he asked, his voice laced with concern. A normal person would have felt bad over deceiving someone he loved on so special a day in so effective a way, but my stomach was doing cartwheels of joy at how perfect my deception was. "Oh, Joe," I said, dramatically throwing my self down on the front steps of my apartment building, "this has been the worst day of my life!" And I launched into some wildly careening story of a terrible computer snafu that lost a really important paper, of a torrid confrontation with a superior at work, and other such little trifles that added up to nothing all-too-serious but just enough to elicit the sympathetic (and totally unsuspecting) response I was hoping for. When I had finished my various tales of woe, Joe put his arm around me and gently tousled my hair. "It's okay," he said. "We'll go out somewhere quiet tonight and you can forget all about it."

"Our anniversary!" I wailed as I stood up. "I *did* forget all about it!" I peered into my lover's gentle brown eyes. "I'm sorry, honey," I said. "I didn't even wrap your presents!"

"That's okay," he replied bravely, shrugging his shoulders gamely, though I could tell my admission had stung him just a bit.

Inside, every neuron in my being was gloating on all cylinders. This was going perfectly! I couldn't wait for the look on his face when he opened my apartment door!

And then Joe said something that threatened to ruin the entire surprise.

"Why are you wearing your slippers?" he asked.

"Huh-what?" I replied, hastily looking at my feet.

"Your slippers I got you last Christmas," he said. "Why are you wearing them? Did you walk home in them?"

With mounting horror I realized that in my haste at Joe's early arrival I had neglected to slip off my favorite household footwear and put on a pair of sneakers. I froze. What the hell kind of lie could I come up with to cover wearing slippers outdoors, not to mention walking all over Christendom in them?

Instinct took over. I burst into tears again about my horrible day. I sputtered out a tale about how I had brought my slippers to work to be comfortable and had forgotten to take them off and now they were probably ruined and I was *soo* distraught from my terrible day I hadn't even noticed them, etcetera, etcetera, etcetera. Frankly, the story was none-too-convincing but the acting was good enough to get the job done. We walked up to my second-floor abode. "Oh, crap!" I exclaimed. "I forgot to get my mail! Here, take the keys—I'll meet you inside in a second." I pretended to walk back down the stairs as Joe fumbled with my pesky lock and opened the door to Christmas in July.

His immediate reaction was silence—a stunned, and I hoped, happy silence. It occurred to me that perhaps I had carried my little charade too far and that Joe might be a bit perturbed at my deceptions. But then he did something that in our previous two years I had never seen him do.

He burst into tears.

We're not just talking a few fat droplets rolling down his cheeks, the kind of tears I often shed during the climactic triumphant moment of really bad movies or every time I see that Folgers coffee commercial where the college student comes home from Christmas and wakes his entire family by making coffee. No, I'm talking unabashed weeping, streams of tears flooding out of his eyes. I wrapped my arms around him and put his face to my shoulder. For a full ten minutes I held him like this, and I knew—I *knew*—right then and there I knew that every second of frantic work I had put into this surprise was worth it. Actually, I never had any doubt it was worth it—never had any doubt *he* was worth it—but this reaction was certainly the best anniversary present I could have asked for.

"No one," he finally sputtered, when he could manage to put together enough words to string a sentence, "no one in my life has ever done anything like this for me. Nothing even comes close, really." And the tears sprang anew as I wrapped my arms around him again. He didn't have to speak. He didn't have to say a word. He'd already said it all.

Everything else may seem anticlimactic, but the evening went perfectly from that point on. Dinner was a great success. (I have since and still do make him all those dishes, and have perfected that sauce into what has become my signature dish.) As a last surprise, Joe found the card when we were clearing away the dishes. I myself had forgot all about it. Opening it, he saw that I had hurriedly writ, in my left-handed, serial-killer scrawl, "Every day with you is Christmas day for me." That earned me a few fresh tears and one long, satisfying kiss.

By the time the fat Santa candle in the center of the table had been reduced to a pair of messy wax boots, we were entwined together on my living room couch, the fake plastic and Mylar fire in my stone-carved fireplace adding one last romantic, wintry touch to the night. As Joe took my hand and moved me toward my bed (thank God I had left it clear of debris), he said to me, "You know, maybe this is how our anniversaries should go from now on. Every other year one person will do something big for the other. I did last year, you did this year, so that means I go again next year. What do you think?"

I smiled my assent. "Sounds perfect," I said, kissing him on the lips and allowing myself to be dragged onto the bed. Still, even as Joe pulled me close to him, I secretly thought to myself, *there is no way he'll ever be able to top this next year. This was just too good.*

But then, on our third anniversary, Joe did manage to one-up me.

He proposed.

MEMORABLE
MOMENTS

DIAMONDS AMONG THE RUST

STEPHEN OSBORNE

THERE'S SOMETHING MAGICAL about the first days of living together. Greg and I had been together only three months when we decided to take that frightening and potentially dangerous leap into cohabitation. The first night, I knew it had been the right decision. I found everything he did to be cute as hell, from the rather strange way he brushed his teeth (just how did he get it to foam like that?) to the adorable little grunt he always let out as he tugged on his high-top basketball shoes. I was in love with him as much on day ninety-five of the relationship as I had been on day one. I loved everything about him, even the pronounced overbite he hated with a passion. Perfection is so boring. Besides, my crooked nose and his overbite complemented each other wonderfully.

In many ways the timing of moving in together sucked. I had just changed jobs, so the bank balance wasn't healthy by any means. Greg had only recently started to work at a local pizza joint after a long period of Sorry We're Not Hiring Right Now, so he was in worse financial shape than I was. We had to scrape together every penny we had just to pay the first month's rent plus the security deposit, leaving basically nothing left for food that first week. Luckily Greg was allowed free pizza from work, so as long as we could stand a diet of pepperoni pies for a week, we'd live.

I had to suppress my excitement the entire time we were moving in the worn and in some cases patched furniture his mother had given us. Not only was I looking forward to jumping his bones in our very own place, but weeks earlier I had purchased tickets to a Joan Baez concert. I had originally planned on going with one of the girls from work, but she had started to date some Neanderthal who wasn't comfortable with her going out with another guy, gay or not. I had yet to tell Greg the ticket was up for grabs.

We finally got unpacked enough that we could say we actually lived there. Greg collapsed onto his mom's ugly red couch and let out a long breath. "I'm done for the day. I can't even look at another box. We can finish up tomorrow night."

I sat down next to him, snuggling in. It's not easy to snuggle in to someone who's not even five and a half feet when you're over six feet, but I managed it. I gazed into his soulful brown eyes. "Would it be alright if we waited an extra day? Remember, I told you about that Joan Baez concert . . . ?"

"Oh, that's right," he said, putting his arm around me. "She's that folksinger you and Jenny are going to see."

He was younger than me, so I forgave him for the offhand "that folksinger" comment. At that time, I would have forgiven him nearly anything. "You say it like she's just any folksinger. She's THE folksinger. You look up folksinger in the dictionary, there's her picture."

Greg frowned. "And what songs would I know of hers again?"

"'Diamonds and Rust', 'The Night They Drove Old Dixie Down' . . . Good God, I know you're young, but where the hell have you been? Anyway, Jenny can't go, so I wondered if you'd go with me."

He shrugged. "Sure. Why not? The tickets are already paid for, aren't they?"

Not exactly the effusive answer I was hoping for, but I figured he was too tired from moving to be more responsive. I pulled him close and kissed those sweet lips. "You'll love her, just wait and see."

I could feel his lips turning to a smile even as we kissed. "I'm sure I will," he replied, before his tongue found its way into my mouth. Discussion of any subject, including concerts, was tabled for the rest of the night.

It would have been nice to go out to a comfy restaurant before the concert and share a romantic dinner, but funds wouldn't allow for that. It was my day off, so I spent some time making our chipped and stained dining table look nice while Greg was off spreading cheese and sauce over dough. Our dinner would be—surprise!—a pizza he'd bring home. I managed to find some candles and cheap candleholders to adorn the table. As I was adding the finishing touches, there was a knock at the door. It was Jason, Greg's younger brother, bringing with him another donated piece of furniture from their mother. It was a Tiffany-style lamp, hideous and kitschy, but we needed a lamp desperately so I gushed over it.

"Yeah, well, don't get too excited," Jason warned. "The cord was smashed under our couch for ages so the light just tends to shut off every now and then. Plus, it's ugly as fuck."

"It's definitely ugly, but what the hell?" I said. "Thank your mother anyway."

Jason eyed the table. "Special night?" He wasn't really comfortable with his brother being gay, but at least he was trying. Every now and then, though, he'd say something like, "special night?" with a slightly disparaging tone, like we really didn't deserve a special night.

"We're going to a Joan Baez concert."

"Who?"

If he wasn't a soccer player who could whoop my ass, I'd have kicked him. "Never mind."

Fortunately, Greg came home right then, saving me from further strained conversation. He kissed me lightly on the cheek, earning a frown from Jason, and then saw the table, complete with lit candles. "Oh!" he said. There was no trace of irony in his voice. He truly thought it was beautiful. "That looks so nice!"

That was one of the things I loved about Greg: the simplest things pleased or excited him. One of the first nights we spent together, we sat in front of the TV watching an episode of *Star Trek: The Next Generation*. In the episode, the Enterprise blows up just before the opening credits. Greg was beside himself, mouth open in shock. "Oh my God!" I laughed and held him close, telling him, "Honey, the show's just started. Something tells me everything's going to be all right."

Jason didn't linger long. He never did. "Enjoy your concert," he muttered before leaving. I'm sure he thought, since he'd never heard of Joan Baez, that it must be some sort of gay thing.

Greg and I sat next to each other to eat. We both were sort of touchy-feely, and liked to have our knees touch while we chowed down. Greg still smelled of grease and pepperoni from work, but I didn't care.

Our feast finished, I ushered Greg into the shower. I'm one of those people who can be ready to go in five minutes. Greg took forever. He had long, nearly girlish brown hair, and it had to be perfect. Jeans had to fit tight and show off his cute little butt just right. I finally got him under the water, then went to our bedroom to find an outfit for him to wear. He'd just try it on, spend minutes in front of the mirror contemplating how it fit before shaking his head and putting on something else, but I figured I might as well get the process started.

He was just starting to lather up when he called out, "Don't you want to join me?"

I was in the next room and could barely hear him. "What?"

"We live together now," he shouted. "Doesn't that mean showering together?"

I stepped into the bathroom. "We'll get distracted and be late for the show."

"I'll be good. I promise."

In no time flat I was undressed and had stepped into the shower with him. We held each other and kissed. I got some of the water from the shower as well as some of his hair in my mouth, but it was one of the most memorable kisses in my whole life.

We somehow managed to get into the Death Trap with plenty

of time to spare. The Death Trap was an old Magnum on its last legs. The brakes were bad, it leaked oil, and no amount of aromatic pine trees would ever get the smell of Hardee's out of it, but it hadn't cost me a dime so I couldn't complain. We didn't actually use it much since we knew it was going to fall apart any second, and there was no way we could afford to fix it. I rode the bus to work and Greg was within walking distance of the pizza place, so the Death Trap had just sat in front of my apartment. Now it had a new home disgracing the parking lot of our new place. There was probably enough gas to get us downtown to the show and back. Probably.

Greg buckled himself into the passenger seat and we started off. Once out on the road he grabbed my right hand and held it, like he always did. At that time, I was still getting used to the idea of holding hands while driving. I'd always been one of those drivers who keeps his hands at ten and two, just like a good little driver's ed student. But when given the choice of engaging in electric contact with the guy you love or being a model driver, there's no contest. We held hands all the way down to 16th Street, when disaster struck.

The car began to lurch and was making some fairly horrible noises. I disengaged my hand and put it back on the wheel, somehow feeling that both hands in place would make the car behave better. It didn't. The engine sputtered and nearly died at the light.

Greg shot me a worried look. "That doesn't sound good."

"No, it doesn't." I pulled into a parking lot next to one of our favorite gay bars. The Death Trap didn't sound like it was going to go another ten feet. I came to a stop and didn't even have to shut off the engine. The car died right then and there.

"What do you think it is?" Greg asked.

"I know about as much about cars as you do," I replied. "I know that you put the key in this thingy and turn it. After that, it's all a mystery to me." I tried to restart the engine. Nothing doing. The Death Trap had given up the ghost.

"What are we going to do?" Greg asked. "Is it out of gas?"

It still had gas, just no life. "I don't know. I guess we'll have to walk the rest of the way."

The Murat Auditorium, where the concert was being held, was still a good ten blocks away. We'd have to haul ass to get there in time. I tried the car one last time. It was silent. Greg got out, looking like he'd just had a brainstorm. "Come on, let's get going. Leave the keys."

"What? Leave the keys? Are you crazy?"

He looked at me like I was stupid. "Can we afford to repair it?"

"No."

"Do we even need the stupid thing?"

"Not really."

"Leave the keys. Trust me on this."

I left the keys in the ignition and got out of the car. He grabbed my hand and we started down the street, walking fast. The fast pace wasn't just to get to the show in time. Even with the gay bars in the area, downtown Indianapolis isn't the safest place for two guys to hold hands in public. If someone wanted to give us grief, at least they'd have to keep pace with us.

Greg wouldn't say anything else about the car, and frankly we didn't waste much breath on talking. I don't know how we did it, but we actually got to the door of the Murat before showtime. We were out of breath and sweaty, but we were there.

Our seats were fantastic. Third row from the stage, right in the center. We'd barely sat down before the lights dimmed.

I'd loved Joan Baez ever since I'd heard "The Night They Drove Old Dixie Down" on the radio those many years ago. I was slightly concerned at how Greg would react to her music. While he enjoyed music from before his time (the sixties and seventies) his tastes went more to The Doors and Jim Morrison. I needn't have worried. Two songs into Joan's set he leaned into me, grabbing my hand. "She's wonderful!" he gushed.

We held hands through the rest of the show. No one around us seemed to care. When Joan got to "Diamonds and Rust", I snuck a look over at Greg. He was listening raptly, mouth open. As the song progressed he began to tear up. "That's fucking beautiful, man," he whispered to me.

Yeah, it was. So was he. I tightened my grip on his hand.

The show ended and we reluctantly stood up. The rest of the crowd headed out to their cars or whatever. I wasn't sure what we were going to do, since I didn't even know if the bus we'd need to get back home ran that late. A cab would be out of the question.

"I've got it all figured out," Greg insisted. "We just need to find a pay phone."

There was one on the street near the Murat. Greg inserted one of our last precious quarters and punched in some numbers. "Mom?" he said, his voice thin and reedy. "You're not going to believe what just happened to Stephen and me. Our fucking car got stolen!"

Now it was time for my mouth to drop open.

Greg managed to sound like he was crying. "Yeah, we were here downtown, we come out of the Murat and our frickin' car's not where it was! Can you believe someone would steal that piece of shit?"

He listened for a few moments, then muttered, "Thanks, Mom. I love you." He hung up and grinned at me. "We just got us a new car."

"What?" I was sure I hadn't heard right.

"Mom and Dad have that old Impala they never use. I figured they'd give it to us if they knew we didn't have a car any longer. Jason's going to come down and get us in it. Then we take him home and drive to our apartment in a car that actually has brakes."

"But . . . we . . . really do still have a car. It's up at 16th Street . . ."

"No, we don't. It was stolen. Jeesh, sometimes I worry about you."

We made a vow, there under a streetlamp, that we'd never reveal to Greg's mom the truth about the car. For all intents and purposes, the car had been stolen. And in a way, it had been. We checked a couple of days later. The car was no longer in the parking lot. Either someone managed to get it going, or it was towed. All we know is that we never heard about the Death Trap again. And that secret made a special night even more wonderful somehow, because now Greg and I were partners in a shared lie. A lie that we've never spoken about.

Until now, that is.

SECOND NIGHT

EZRA REDEAGLE WHITMAN

THERE ARE MOMENTS about major decisions I've made in my life when I teeter between regret and conviction; moments of panic-stricken paddling in deep water hoping to claw myself upon a rock to push the water from lungs and take a saving breath. I'm a dreamer, a wanderer, a curious learner, and stubborn—if not a little naïve—about living an unhurried, border-hopping life. Maybe I'm a bit of an undercover lunatic in pursuit of love, laughter, good food, and similar souls. It's my own loyalty to this type of living that places me in situations where I need to look hard for signs of payoff, to avoid having to give in to a more conventional life strapped to a narrower path.

One such instance took place during a date with Ian, my boyfriend, after moving back to San Jose, Costa Rica to be with him. I was in love. Multilingual, intellectually seasoned, and well traveled, Ian embodied everything I had wanted to develop within myself. He also remained loyal to his own boyhood tendencies to find inspiration and fun in the world around him. I had lived in Costa Rica before, but only as an exchange student for a brief few months, which was when we first met. After a long and trying eight-month separation and countless letters, I had decided to move back and attend the university there as a full-time student. I was nervous entering a Spanish-speaking institution and my skills, although decent, were shy of that required for sophisticated university rhetoric. Nevertheless, Ian, an accomplished language instructor, was

a great resource, and I considered the language barrier an exciting challenge. That's just the kind of learner I am—sink or swim.
That first night there, I'll have you know, was reserved for aching lovers. We came straight to his apartment from the airport
and warmed the house with our own blatant version of a proper
reception. The next evening, however, we opted for something
more formal. We spent some time getting dressed and ready, and
I remember so well how damned good he looked that night: a thin
black sweater a little snug around his arms and across his chest, a
fun pair of jeans that complemented his rounded backside where
the pockets clung to the rise and fall there as he walked; my *ma-
cuco*, a word used to describe someone with some width, not heavy
or overdeveloped, but well fed and filled out. It has always struck
me as such a delicious word.

As we left his apartment, he explained to me which key to use
for each lock: one for the door, another for the gate at the end of
a small walkway, and finally the big gate that opened out to the
quiet street. Stepping out into his neighborhood at dusk felt like
the rising of a curtain to reveal a painted scene upon stage—the
surreal colors and stacked slant of the buildings—something I was
forced to believe by actually being there. The pink sun, setting in
the Pacific, tinged the haze above downtown San Jose and scattered its light like a screen over the houses and trees, while setting
ablaze plump clouds that approached from the north.

The houses here were larger than in other *barrios* I had been
to, and Ian told me it was due to old money, from an older neighborhood built on the first of wide, rolling hills to the east of
downtown, between the city and university districts. We walked
down the middle of the wide, flat streets without so much as a taxi
rolling by to return someone from the supermarket. Tall black
rails fenced in the yards like cages protecting the homes from
intruders, and bars had been bolted across every window. It wasn't
that the area was dangerous or violent, but the urban culture had
developed into a cautious one, a bustling system of anonymity
and scattered crime with a far-from-efficient police force. Crime

lurked in the minds of everyone when outside their home, Ian explained. I wondered how easy it would be, as a newcomer, to slip into careless habits with so much beauty around: the sweet cool of the fickle weather, the fragrant red flowers in constant bloom spilling through the black rail fencing, the giant green trees heavy with bantering flocks of birds—disarming in the romantic sense for a visiting traveler. What I had envisioned of a tropical urban scene was just this: the cracked streets, clipped hedges along the sidewalks, the leafy and manicured yards, mixed with the sporadic hum of electric gates opening for cars to slip into the safety of their garages. It was a land of soccer kings and gaudy television shows, where flat-roofed, modern homes stood next to old, tin-roofed, pastel-colored houses with the front doors right up off the sidewalks. Superheroes could exist in such splendid storybook urban landscapes.

The twenty-minute stroll to his favorite restaurant brought us a few blocks from downtown, and when we arrived he waved to a couple of friends there for dinner as well. After we were seated, one friend approached our table. They exchanged pleasantries and Ian introduced me. Upon hearing my name and accent, he asked where I was from, how long I'd be in the country, and of course how Ian and I had met. A few moments later, his friend wished us well and returned to his own table. Ian and I eyed each other over our menus and laughed at the attention received. It was times like this that the fun side of our connection surged. We'd discussed before how gays can be remarkably curious, and how to satisfy that curiosity a certain amount of calculation takes place—like this friend of his who had been sent by the other table to probe for information on me. Ian claimed there were circles of boys with not-so-subtle ways to either flirt or get information; and though there wasn't always any harm intended, the resulting conversation tends to be one bordering cynicism as they wonder who the new boy toy is, where he's from, how serious the relationship is, and whether or not they'll see him out at the bars. Boys can be so blatant sometimes, and I have accepted this as something comical, a little annoying at times, but ultimately entertaining. Ian under-stood me in that sense. We wanted to be full of love, untouchable by unnecessary negativity, and just enjoy everything we could by limiting any tendency to "awfulize" situations or people, however impossible that may sound. So far, our attempts to do so always seemed much more enjoyable than the alternative.

Ian was right. It was a great restaurant. Huge, hand-painted lilies and irises sprawled the walls and ceiling, a fountain trickled near the entrance to a patio, and the dim lighting gave everyone a smooth glow. The candle at our table trembled with the breeze through the windows, and cast a swaying shadow across Ian's smil-ing face. A busy night, our food came after our third glass of wine, and by then we had both felt its effect flushing our cheeks. It was just Ian and me inside that thin orb cast by our lone candle and I held on to every word he said, sputtered my responses, laughed when he imitated eccentric people we had met while in Italy. At one point, I started teasing him about the Batman costume I had found in his spare closet when I unpacked my clothes. The costume had been made by his mother when he was in grade school, and he was so impressed and later so touched by his mom's handy work that he'd kept the costume all these years. A diehard fan of Batman and Robin, Ian was convinced they had some sort of torrid goings on when alone in the Bat Cave. He had, of course, outgrown the costume, but I begged him to slip the mask over his face, just to see if it would still fit, but he was too embarrassed to do it.

In that warm, sort of lustrous and muted moment between the two of us, as I sat there devouring more than my share of olive bread and tortellini, I felt that bloat of contentment when every-thing is how you want it to be. When everything, however fleet-ing, is in sync.

We were accustomed to great dates; fabulous dates in fact, full of conversation, laughter, and good food. Dates spanning those first few magical moments sitting at cafes in his neighborhood when we first met, the scattered telephone dates while I was back in the States, and even our own classic *Meet Me in Rome* adventure we had taken after I had left Costa Rica the first time.

I was still uneasy about my decision to leave all the comforts of home and try this new life. Would I make it in the university? Was it the right decision? Would I run out of savings? How would I get a job as a foreigner? I told him that only when the plane jolted against the runway and all the Costa Rican passengers returning home clapped and cheered the plane's touchdown, did the magnitude of my decision hit me: I was a new arrival, a foreigner, and completely on my own. He slowed his chewing, gazed concerned into the candle, and wrapped his palm around one of my fingers the way a kid in a store might. Looking like a little boy with his sideways grin, even with his broad shoulders and grown-up clothes, he told me he'd do whatever it took to make me feel at home. I loved him so much for it.

We left the restaurant and strolled up the slant of a rickety road, passing the gated doorways of rectangular, pastel-colored homes built flush against one another. We retraced our path for a few blocks down a well-lit street, which ended at a small hospital looming over the rest of the neighborhood atop the crest of the sloping block. The lights of the hospital blazed against the dark sky, and the clouds had shifted south, giving way to faint stars teasing the upper heights of the hospital's aura. Ian, both giddy on wine and eager to show another feature of the neighborhood, took me a block over to a quiet tree-lined street where single streetlamps marked each intersection. The stars shone brighter, speckling the sky like a forceful spatter against black. Ian explained how this road clipped the edge of the broad knoll where his neighborhood sat and allowed a view of the constellations on cloudless nights. Ian pointed some out, at times struggling with their English translations even though his English was perfect, and I needed to orient myself to their altered positioning since I was now closer to the equator.

The idea of me being this far from home and seeing the same constellations from a new angle reminded me of the lives that would continue at home without me. Home still existed regardless of the intensity and singularity I felt venturing out in a new, unfamiliar world. Knowing that home was far beyond the Pacific ridge of mountains at the outer side of the central valley, but still under the same constellations, helped me understand that those from my old life, my beloved family, continued with their own journeys. I found comfort in this notion of simultaneity and how everything familiar to me paralleled everything new, and how in some way I lived both. At times of great stress it helps to be reminded of the fleeting nature of all things, to remember how insignificant a single celestial body is compared to the infinite amount of others to consider. If I wanted to live a life that brought me the joy and satisfaction I craved, then it could be possible, it could be allowed because there was nothing grandiose about my existence. It was all a matter of perspective.

I spread my arms in the middle of the street, tilted my head back, and spun twice in slow circles, watching the stars leave fuzzy trails against the film of sky. I accepted the charm of everything, accepted this seeming invitation to this new life, and released a wine-laced sigh. I glanced at Ian who gazed toward the horizon at the far side of the city, trying to calculate which stars or planets would present themselves in the coming months. He mumbled to himself and I asked him to speak up. He laughed, returned his gaze to the sky above us, and shot a look down the street. I caught his double take, saw his smile dissipate as he stopped mid-sentence and fixed his gaze forward.

I turned to look down the street, where a block away three figures approached. They merged from one side of the street toward our projected path. Ian told me in a flat voice, "Get ready to run." An eerie calm set around us, and the buzz of a lone streetlamp humming above me was the last I remember before they came upon us and barked a slur of orders and threats that I hardly understood.

I ran. A moist hand clawed at my neck then slipped off as I flung my shoulder, but not even half a block away I glanced behind me to see Ian yanked backward by the collar of his sweater.

All three closed in around him and I had no choice but to return.

"*Mae, OK, mae. Tranqilo. Suélteme, mae. ¿Qúe quieren? Les doy lo que quieran.*" Ian shot his elbows to both sides telling them to mellow out and he'd cooperate.

When I approached, Ian looked at me with tearful eyes. One of the guys prodded my pockets, and I stood there with my hands exposed showing no fight. Another yelled close to my face, lifted a knife above his shoulder. I looked at the taut forearm, followed it to the raised tendons below his wrist, and felt a chill along my limbs, not knowing when he might jerk under the quivering tension and carve the knife downward—its rusty blade—through the air and into my hands, my stomach. The one prodding my jeans slipped my wallet from the left front pocket and stepped back.

"*Por favor, toma el dinero, pero dejame el resto . . . es que . . . es que—*" I sputtered a plea for him to leave me at least my wallet. My ID and credit cards would have been useless to him.

He opened my wallet, took what little cash I had in there, and tossed the wallet at my chest; it fell flat against the pavement.

The others continued with Ian and he lifted his sleeve to unfasten his watch. The one with my money remained quiet as I watched how they treated Ian, focusing on the one with the knife. I'm still unsure why he did it—frustration, guilt, fright, nerves?— but the one who took my money jabbed a bony fist at my face and caught me on the brow. My head snapped to the side and I returned a bewildered, rabid stare. Whether he thought I'd run or drop cold to the ground, he was alarmed to see me not so much as blink. It was sheer adrenaline, that frantic, icy response to fright that kept me from feeling any pain, and I'm also sure that it was a weak hit. He appeared too malnourished to produce much force.

He hopped back and resurged with more yelling; something about having a knife in his pocket. I knew he was bluffing, but I had to remind myself of the others, otherwise the pig-headedness inherited from my dad would have taken over. The less reasonable side of my nature would have prompted me to grab him by his throat, pull the weight of his body toward me, and shove his head in the opposite direction, watching him spin hard against the ground. I clenched a clammy hand into a tight fist, digging the nails into my palm, trying to find some way to vent the anger tightening my windpipe.

Once Ian surrendered his watch, they gave us a final shove, turned, ran down the block, and slipped around a corner. We returned to the main road a block over, where our pace remained constant, not quite a jog, but a hurried, noiseless gait. I dragged a hand across my eyes to keep the tears from falling, and Ian glanced at my face. His chin quivered as he whispered that he was sorry. To my mind he owed me no apology, but I know my silence implied that my acceptance thereof was up for review until further notice. I tried to find a way to control the urge I had to yell and kick and pound my fists bloody against the pavement like a madman. I hated this sense of defeat and submission, and my insides boiled at the thought that I allowed this to happen a mere twenty-four hours after my arrival.

By the time we reached his gate and had slipped down the dark corridor to his front door, I had calmed down some and found it in me to tell him he had nothing to be sorry for. We sat in silence at his dining table, gazing out to his patio where lush ferns swayed beneath a downdraft spinning off the roof. The tension of my jaw loosened after a few more moments; I breathed out a long sigh and felt my shoulders go limp as I sat back in the chair. Ian sat opposite me and when I looked at him, he grabbed my hand, kissed my palm, and blew against the still damp spaces between my fingers. His breath felt cool against the perspiration there and I closed my eyes to its relief. A tear rolled down my face and I pressed a shoulder against my cheek to let it seep into my shirt. I glanced at Ian's stretched collar, grasped his other hand, and held it to my face. I wondered then if I had made the right decision of moving there.

It seems to be during the aftermath of something tragic when the simplest reality feels the most accurate. I just didn't belong there, especially if I was to forfeit the freedom of stargazing on a lonely street in order to stay safe. That wasn't my idea of a life. Maybe my presence had caused Ian to make the wrong decision about diverting from the busier street so we could take a lover's walk. I began questioning myself then, about how many other poor but-they-seemed-good-at-the-time decisions he would make with me in his life. I began to wonder if this love distorted our view of what entailed prudent choices in our lives. I wondered if my stay needed to be nothing more than a visit, if I should return home.

"I'm going to get out of these clothes," Ian said.

He left to his bedroom and I heard his shoes drop against the hardwood floor. I stood and turned on the TV, not really paying attention to what was on. I settled onto his sofa and lifted a magazine off the coffee table. It was the latest issue of *Out*, and I came upon a center fashion spread in black and white of two young men on the verge of an impassioned kiss, their disheveled clothes apparently the hottest look for gay fashion at the time. I had come out of the closet only a year prior, so things like *Out* magazine were still new to me, and the whole fantasy of living a gay life, learning a gay culture, having a partner, and leaning against him in disheveled clothes was what I wanted more than anything at that point in my life. It saddened me and I felt cheated to think I might have to pass this one up for something closer to home. The anger and the tears resurfaced and I looked up at the TV but only saw blurry images roll back and forth.

I heard Ian in the back room. I wasn't sure what he was doing, but I figured he might have opted for a shower and was going through the linen closet. I didn't really pay attention until he called out my name. I wiped my eyes and squirmed about the sofa to hang over the armrest and peer around the corner. He stood in the doorway wearing his undershirt and black boxer briefs. The mask of the Batman costume was stretched over his head, a pitiful ear bent at an awkward angle and the cape barely covering one shoulder. His dark eyes took most of the space in the eyeholes but were situated toward the inner corners, making him look cross-eyed.

"Let's go get us some bad guys," he said.

I doubled over the armrest, felt the blood rush to my face as my diaphragm tightened and my laughter spilled out in loud waves. I slid from the sofa to my knees on the floor and crawled around the corner. When I stood, Ian had met me and gave me a long warm hug. When I pushed him back to get a second look I started laughing again; I'm sure he had no idea how crossed-eyed he looked, especially when he smiled.

"You look so cute!" I told him.

"Let's see someone mess with us now, huh?" he said.

The thought of him out in public like this, perhaps sitting in the back seat of the bus with a nonchalant gaze fixed forward, made me laugh so hard I started crying. The tears poured, and I don't know if they were sour from pent up anger or sweet with the love I felt in that moment. I just let them go. I set my weight against Ian's chest and he held me there while my laughter eased and my tears ran dry.

That's when I found the rock during my frantic paddling in deep waters. The moment lingered like a blinking cursor on a white screen, waiting for a decision, and there was Ian showing me plainly who he was, as if to say *this is me, this is my life, my boyhood dreams*. It was that moment that convinced me I was in the right place—that fabulous date my second night in a new life—and whispered to me of love and laughter, and the possibility of boyhood dreams and superheroes in this urban landscape.

GAY PRIDE PARTY

JAY STARRE

THAT AUGUST LONG weekend was hot. Vancouver is a beach city, but only basks in true heat for a few short weeks in August, and sometimes not even then. But that weekend could not have been more perfect.

A light breeze off English Bay lessened the impact of the 28 degrees Celsius, while not a cloud in the sky had myriad gay boys and lesbians huddling in the shade of the cherry trees and oaks that lined Denman Street and Pacific. Soon, the Gay Pride Parade would wend its way along those streets to the cheers of several hundred thousand onlookers.

Sun and heat meant a lot of skin, no bad thing for a gay pride celebration. The theme that year was something gaudy and shallow and every float and marching entrant went all out to show its colours.

I was with a group of buddies, but my mind was elsewhere. Not even the hottest scantily clad studs prancing by with water guns were able to distract me from my focus.

Robbie noticed. "Eyes only for your new sweetie?"

Not even that teasing laughter distracted me. It was true, though. I was hoping to see Damon.

We'd had sex for the first time only two days ago, and it had gone so far beyond merely fucking, I was still in a daze from it. Damon and I had only met three weeks earlier at the city's outdoor pool. We both swam lengths, and both struggled at the end of the fifty meters to catch our breath. He reached over the lane rope and offered a friendly handshake.

"I'm Damon."

That day had been glorious and sunny, too. The next time we ran into each other at the pool, he came home with me and we fucked our brains out in my cramped bedroom-office in the middle of the afternoon.

The two days since had gone by with one phone call and a promise to meet today. Gay Pride Day. Among three hundred thousand other milling and cruising celebrants, it was a slim chance we would run into each other. What I really wanted to do was to run home and wait by the phone for his call.

But I was a grown man, forty-eight that year, and supposedly well beyond the risk of a silly infatuation running my life. Damon, on the other hand, was only twenty-six, and could be excused his own silly infatuation. If he was truly infatuated, too.

I peeled down to shorts and sandals, never one to be ashamed of a gym-built body and a good tan. I certainly wasn't alone, as other men attempted to attract and mesmerize with their own muscles. Vancouver is shallow that way, fit bodies a must in the hierarchy of who gets laid and who doesn't.

The drag queens pranced by, in all their fabulous glory, the retailers with their floats proclaiming their love for gay dollars, and even the religious groups offering their equally loving embrace. Banks, gyms, dance clubs, the police, the fire department, and even the premier of the province paraded by to cheers and clapping.

The parade itself is a liberating experience, with so many gay men and women out there in massive crowds shouting their defiant message of pride in themselves. I always loved it. But that day, the usual high was heightened by turmoil. Would I see Damon? Was there more to our meeting besides a pleasant chat at the pool and an uninhibited afternoon of nasty and exciting sex?

The parade ended in a melee at the beach with music and local celebrities and more cruising. All those thousands crammed into a few hectares of grass and sea wall, pushing against each other, grinning, winking, offering sultry looks . . . usually I revelled in it.

But where was Damon? Would I see him in the massive crowd? I still wanted to rush home and wait for a call, but my buddies were having a great time and weren't about to let me go just yet. A moment later, I was glad they hadn't.

"Jay! There you are. I couldn't miss you with that tan and that awesome chest."

Damon materialized out of the tens of thousands, suddenly in front of me. I beamed, unable to pretend I wasn't overjoyed at seeing him. We hugged, his shorter body sun-warm in my arms. I felt his stocky form against mine, tempted in a moment of sudden lust to drop my hands and grope his sexy round ass. I behaved, and he kissed my cheek and grinned as we came apart.

That was one of the great things about Gay Pride Day: men kiss and hug other men without the least inhibition, in broad daylight, in public, on crowded streets. It's as if a magical wand had been waved over the world and suddenly it was normal and wonderful for men to be affectionate to each other in front of all.

"I'm with my friends, over there," he said, pointing. "Can we meet in an hour? Around two?"

Damon sounded eager and happy to see me, which was exactly what I needed. I agreed and let him go, watching him disappear back into the multitude. That ass! Smooth legs, very tan, and a small head on broad shoulders, neatly cropped auburn hair over almost elfin ears. From the back, he was just as beautiful as from the front.

I was still basking in his kiss and the feel of his arms around me when I faced my buddies.

They had been ignoring me before that, intent on cruising the crowds and copping free hugs whenever possible. But now it seemed like all eyes were on me.

"Well, well, Jay. You've caught yourself a cute little chicken," Robbie smirked and the others laughed.

They had been unanimous in their judgment about our age difference. Fine for a quick fuck, but a relationship? Not likely to work, they all had said. I myself couldn't care less about age. I got along well with everyone. Otherwise, I wouldn't have shaken hands with Damon in the first place and spent so much time chatting with him at the pool before we hit the sack.

I was euphoric, and their undisguised derision hardly mattered to me. I actually tingled from Damon's touch. It had been like that from our first handshake. There was something electric between us, physically at least. Was there more? It seemed so to me.

The truth is, I was open to a relationship. I was open to love. I knew it, had known it for some time. I had just been waiting for lightning to strike. Open to love, to me, just meant not being afraid to take a risk. Not judging, or making snap decisions. Just let it happen. If it works, a miracle has occurred.

Then, on a brilliant summer afternoon, a cute young swimmer had reached across the lane rope and offered me his hand. I was open to him that day. My heart was bare, and I'm sure my smile betrayed me.

Two o'clock rolled around and Damon did not show up. I wasn't worried yet. The crowds on the grass below were still large and there was a lot to see. Men from all over Canada, and the US—and the world for that matter—walked around in a mesmerizing mix of semi-naked, rainbow-necklace-bedecked, and painted glory.

On a sunny day in a rain-washed city, everyone smiles. On Gay Pride Day, even backstabbing enemies smile and hug and pretend all is forgiven. A cumulative joy permeates everything, and I was content to wait for Damon for as long as it took. Really, as long as it took.

It took almost half an hour. Later, I was to learn that this was a habit. I was always early for appointments, or on time; he was almost always late.

Damon rushed up to me and we collided in a sweaty hug. I was still holding my shirt rather than wearing it; he was in shorts but wore a sleeveless soccer jersey. He had already told me he was embarrassed by a slight roll of fat around his waist, and was shy about going without a shirt in public.

"I couldn't miss you standing there. Tall and hot and handsome," Damon said with a laugh.

Compliments usually made me uncomfortable, but I bore his with a pleased grin. "So what do you want to do now? Should we just walk around for a while? There's at least ten different parties going on this afternoon."

Vancouver's West End was not only a residential gay ghetto, but also the central club and restaurant location for gay party life. Gay Pride celebrations had been rocking the village since Friday and it was now Sunday; and no sign of party fatigue had yet set in.

There was plenty to do. I didn't care what we did, though, as long as we did it together. That attitude pretty well ensures a good time. Damon's next words echoed my sentiments.

"We'll find something. I'd like to hear some good music and dance maybe, but I'm cool with whatever happens. As long as we can hang out together. Are you mine for the day?"

Damon looked up at me and grinned, reaching out to take my hand as we began to walk down the sidewalk away from the beach. At six feet tall I stood a few inches above him. He had the most beautiful skin, a shade of olive that set off his close-cropped, deep-brown hair and darker-brown arched brows. His small ears, nose, lips, and chin all contributed to his elfin look, which I adored.

He held my hand for a few blocks, which was a surprise. But Damon was affectionate, and had been quick to touch even from that first handshake. As we reached the busier intersection of Davie and Denman, he let go of my hand and I put on my T-shirt.

"You can leave it off if you want, Jay. I like showing you off. I like it when guys look at your chest and envy me my good luck."

Damon's voice was light and teasing. He was not loud spoken or outrageous or pushy, even though he had made the first moves in our dance of getting to know each other. I was easy-going myself and reserved in public. It was a miracle we had actually come together.

I put on my shirt anyway, not really comfortable with everyone staring at my chest. We wandered down the streets, chatting about the weather and the parade and the possibilities for the day.

"There're three dance parties tonight, but they cost around eighty bucks. Too much for music I probably won't like," Damon admitted.

I was pleased that, despite other differences, we were nearly economic equals. He was new to Vancouver, from Toronto, and had only just acquired a retail job at a clothing store for pittance wages. I was a struggling writer and could hardly justify spending a week's food allowance on one night's dance party.

"The clubs will all be busy, and their cover won't be more than twenty bucks," I said.

"The line-ups are going to be huge, though, won't they?"

"Let's just see what happens. I like walking around and looking at the crowds."

We strolled by the first party, at the local recreation center. It was an afternoon tea party with music blasting out into the alley and the men packed so tightly in an outdoor patio I couldn't see how they managed to even move.

"They're all pretty drunk," Damon laughed as we gawked from the alley.

Neither of us drank. Alcohol made me sick, vomiting and all. He just didn't like to be drunk. "I do stupid things and wake up the next day regretting it," he said with a charming laugh.

"I don't need to be drunk to do stupid things and wake up re-gretting it," I admitted.

I am basically an honest person but, like anyone, I want oth-ers to respect or like me. It's easy to say or do what you know the other person will approve of. With Damon, even though I really wanted him to like me, I had been frank and honest right from the start. I wanted him to know me, and to like me for me, too.

We continued on. Even the alleys of the West End were full of happy gay boys in search of the next good time. It was our day to dominate the village, happily proud to be who we were. Damon and I returned to the main drag, Davie Street, and climbed the hill toward the pubs.

There were half a dozen restaurants to nearly every block, and it was easy to choose one for an afternoon snack. Even with all the crowds, we managed to find an outdoor table to claim and munched on our sandwiches with a good view of the party.

Time stood still as that long afternoon rolled on around us.

"This is great. You're not in a rush to do something else, are you?" Damon asked, his smaller hand covering mine on the table between our lunches.

I was in no hurry to go or be anywhere else. Often, when on a date, the expectation is for upcoming sex. I can't say I didn't look at Damon and crave touching him, caressing him, and fucking him, but we had already done that, and done it spectacularly. I really didn't look ahead, merely content to enjoy the moment.

"I don't want the day to end. It's too perfect," I admitted with a blush.

This was not the attitude of most of my buddies, who were constantly worrying about what party they should go to, which place would have the hottest guys, which the best music, what would they miss by being somewhere else? I felt none of that.

We meandered farther up the street, past outdoor patios packed with increasingly inebriated and sunburned men. A few hollered out hellos to me, and I waved back as they checked out my date with speculative eyes. Damon admitted he knew hardly anyone.

We chattered away as we walked. We really didn't know much about each other yet, with only a few hours of conversation behind us. Everything and anything came up.

"I played soccer, tennis, and football as a kid, but had such bad asthma I was in the hospital for weeks at a time. I played football in college, though, for two years. I guess I'm a jock." His soft-spoken admission made us both laugh. I had seen his inhaler at the pool, and had asked about it. I had once been a lifeguard and first aid attendant so I was always alert to that kind of stuff. He had admitted about the asthma then, and dismissed it.

"I've got a football at home," I said. "Maybe we could toss it around one day later this week. I never played on a team, but with four brothers and thirty male cousins, we had our own football team every day."

"Catholics? Me too." We both laughed and Damon took my hand again as we walked. "My ex was Catholic too. We split up almost two years ago now. But we're really good friends still. Brian is older than you by a year or two."

"So you like old men?" I joked.

"Yeah. I'm not really turned on by guys my age. I guess that's weird. But that's me. What about your last boyfriend? He was probably hot, wasn't he?" Damon winked.

"He was cute, and actually he was younger than me by quite a bit. Thirty-five. He was a liar, though. Turned out he was married with three kids and was a pastor for a fundamentalist Christian sect. He said he was leaving his wife. It took me more than six months to finally realize he wasn't going to."

"What a jerk!"

"No. He was stuck in a life he didn't want, and didn't know how to escape it. I loved him and he loved me, but it wasn't going to work out and I had to end it." We had ascended most of Davie Street's hill and I spotted one of the nightclubs ahead. "Hey, what about Numbers? Their party doesn't start until eight so there's no cover charge now. Let's go in and check it out."

There wasn't even a queue outside. A momentary surplus of available parties had offered us the perfect opportunity. Moving from the bright early evening sun to the dimly lit club was a real contrast, but we were prepared for it. The music beat against us like a throbbing hard-on, the DJ above the dance floor doing his best to liven up the audience. The three floors were loud and fairly busy with milling men.

The dance floor was packed. And it was only six o'clock in the evening! It was truly an unusual day. Damon stuck close to me,

the shoving men around us uncaring about whether they separated us or not. Speculative eyes on both of us only drew us closer
together.

"Want to dance?" I asked.

"I have to warn you, Jay. I dance weird. I'm used to dancing at
raves."

"Everyone dances weird," I laughed, pulling him out to the
floor and into the center of the heaving mass of men.

I loved to dance. I played the piano at one time before I turned
my fingers to the computer and writing, and the beat of music always got my blood thrumming and my body gyrating. A remix of
Abba rocked the house, and Damon leaned in to shout in my ear.

"I love this!"

That was good. He had been a little reluctant to dance, and I
wasn't going to keep him out there for more than one song if he
wasn't happy. But one song became an amazing several hours, the
highlight of our day and our date.

Damon bounced up and down as he danced, sort of an enthusiastic hop, which was a little unusual but exactly what they did
at raves. I swayed, rocked, and gyrated like the more mainstream
crowd, but there were plenty of wild and uninhibited dancers on
the floor to make both of us feel like we didn't stand out.

The floor was pretty crowded, so we danced close enough to
touch almost all the time. It took him two songs before he reached
over and stripped off my shirt. "You look so hot like that," he
shouted.

I had danced without a shirt plenty of times, but always fought
a little bit against innate shyness when I did. I sweated like a pig
when I danced, and felt better without some damp rag hanging on
my chest. But nearly half the other men danced without shirts, so
at least I wasn't alone.

The worst part about taking my shirt off was not the way men's
eyes always zeroed in on my chest, which is extremely muscular
and smooth, and tanned when the weather permits. That is a little
unsettling, as they don't look in my eyes but instead at my chest,

as if I didn't have a face. But worse, much worse, is the unexpected seizure of one of my nipples by some passing stranger. I have been pinched and tweaked so many times I have become resigned to it, but I still find it rude.

Damon tweaked my nipples. Right there in the midst of the milling, writhing, sweating, staring crowd of dancing men. Now that I didn't mind, not in the least. What would have irritated me in someone else, was perfectly fine when he did it.

"I love your chest, you know!" he shouted in my ear.

My hands slid from his waist to grope his butt and I shouted back, "I love your ass, you know!"

He kissed me on the cheek, then the ear, and thrust his body against mine, both of us soaked in sweat. We danced on, our hands constantly reaching out to caress each other, to graze over arms, chest, back, hips, butt. He turned around and slid into my arms, grinding that round ass into my crotch as we swayed to the music.

We were oblivious to others, yet aware of them too, as men laughed and nodded to us, but gave us our space. We were a pair, together, in lust or love or heat or whatever, and it was clear to the world.

"I'm so proud to be dancing with you. Everyone is staring at you. You really know how to dance," Damon shouted in my ear, licking the lobe.

I was more realistic. I have muscles, lots of them. Gay men saw the muscles, and the swaying, humping, writhing movement of those muscles. Their eyes were for that body, not me or how I danced. But it didn't matter, because I loved to dance.

I kissed Damon back, on the cheek, then the nose, then the lips. Arms around each other, swaying to remixed Madonna, we kissed.

A kiss can be consuming, as consuming as the moment a cock drives deep inside a willing ass, or a mouth swallows a hard cock to the root, or even as consuming as the moment of body-wracking orgasm we all crave so much. Our kiss was all that. His lips lush and soft, his mouth open to my tongue. His tongue sliding into my mouth. The music throbbed around us, other bodies accidentally bumped ours. Time stood still.

Love invaded and elevated that kiss. Love infused that kiss with lust, with need, with promise, and with hope. We floated in that kiss, a world unto ourselves. We were in love.

We finally left the floor, hand in hand, sweating and grinning. Pushing our way through the packed throng, who now made it almost impossible to move in the jammed club, we headed out the door.

"Had enough?" I gasped out, sweat trickling down into my eyes, the night air suddenly cool and refreshing.

"No. Can I come home with you?"

The date ended in bed, certainly no bad thing. Damon was fun in bed. Afterward he slept cradled in my shoulder, affectionate even in sleep. I drifted off with a smile to the comforting rhythm of his breathing.

It had been the perfect date. The perfect date. Tomorrow, and life, loomed ahead, uncertain but full of possibility.

MY FIRST REAL VALENTINE'S DAY

MICHAEL LUONGO

WHEN I WAS in my early twenties, when I thought of "a date", I didn't think of ones with my own partner. But then I found a partner, and we lived about an hour apart, so we only got to see each other on weekends, mostly, and we treated each of those as a long, precious date.

Completely bored with my life at the time and in a job that didn't allow for much creativity, I made the dates with my boyfriend, who I'll simply call Jake, as adventurous and creative as possible. I loved playing dress-up, and I had both an array of outfits and other odds and ends to transform my apartment into whatever theme I wanted. Once I was a guido hustler, with ripped up jeans, a guinea-T, a leather jacket, and a disgustingly fake gold crucifix hanging over my hairy chest. I waited for Jake on the porch of my building as if I had been hoping any random handsome stranger would come by. We pretended we had never met and made love calling each other Tony and John. Another time, I was an angel, with white feather wings and a loincloth, my apartment strewn with white tulle. Then I was the boyfriend from outer space, this time clothed in silver lamé, the same material draped throughout my bedroom.

Valentine's Day, though, is what I remember the best: our first one together, in 1993. I had been out for a few years, but Jake was my first real boyfriend, hookups of course being quite another story. Everything had been happening so fast, and even now we were only four months into what was to become an almost four-year relationship. Jake was my first love, the first man I had ever truly dated, and so I had nothing to compare it to, to see what was right, what was wrong, to judge if things were proceeding as they should be.

Still, I knew I wanted our first Valentine's Day to be special; I racked my brain for some kind of fantasy setup for the long weekend.

At the time, I managed the housewares lines at a JC Penney's in a suburban shopping mall. We carried a line of Wilton baking products, and along with heart-shaped pans for a cake I'd be making, I bought edible pre-molded frosting hearts meant as cake decorations. My staff was all women about my mother's age who often gave me advice on cooking. They never tried to set me up with their daughters or other women: even with things unspoken, they seemed to know something. Of course, I was sure, too, that the ladies I managed had no idea what I had planned to do with these hearts. They knew Jake, but they didn't quite know at the time exactly how much he meant to me, nor the strangely-fun adventures I often planned for us.

The evening of Valentine's Day, I pulled the petals from dozens of cheap red roses, mixed them with red glitter and tiny plastic hearts, and scattered that blend in a trail from the door to the porch, up the stairs, through the apartment, and into my bedroom where I would be waiting for Jake.

I can't remember if I was wearing red underwear, or if I was completely naked. That much didn't matter. The most important thing was that I had taken the Wilton hearts and pasted them all over my hairy body, using vanilla frosting to glue them in place.

I had tried to time everything right, making sure I did this only shortly before he was supposed to be at my apartment, but for some reason Jake was hours late. I fell asleep on my bed, the frosting drying into flakes over my body, the hearts somehow miraculously still in place. I awoke with Jake leaning over me, looking exhausted. He was wearing an expensive, well-tailored olive suit; his chestnut hair flopped over his forehead.

Jake worked retail, too (jewelry), and men buying last-minute items for their wives meant he had no control over when he left his store. He had a very expensive array of flowers with him. Some were velvety and looked like plants you'd find on a *Star Trek* planet. Next door to his house was a high-end florist, and he was always picking up unique arrangements for me; the thrill of getting flowers was always part of our extended date.

Jake smiled at me as I rubbed my eyes awake, then grabbed for him. At first, he didn't want to give himself up to me, since he was in his suit; there was no way we could kiss without making a mess. After just a single frosting smear, he realized resistance was futile. I forced him out of his jacket and made him eat the hearts off my hairy body, feeling him tongue his way through the flaking frosting. We laughed as I thought to myself that this is what love must mean, since it must have been kind of gross eating them off my very hairy torso, one by one. He peeled off some of the hearts and fed them to me, too, my tongue stuck out like a worshipper waiting for communion. We made a total mess of his clothes, but that was what dry cleaning was for.

I don't remember how long we made love, but we moved from the bed to the floor and back again several times. Dinner for the evening was shot because he was so late, so we decided to go dancing instead. There really was only one place to go: the Den, the local gay dance bar just outside of New Brunswick in New Jersey where I lived at the time. We showered, letting the frosting dissolve off our bodies, and then made love once again, both of us so euphorically in the moment.

I was still in a daze when we arrived at the crowded Den, which was full of men hoping for one last chance at love that evening. All of our single friends were there too, and I said hello to every one of them, leading Jake around as if he were my prize. Yet in the end, I didn't care to talk to anyone, I only wanted to be near Jake.

I wanted to dance all night, or until the music stopped at a way too early 1:30 A.M. I only had eyes for Jake, as we held each other's hands, spinning on the dance floor, looking only at each other, intense, almost insane smiles carved across our faces. At the time, I felt like I was in one of those movies where two people are on the dance floor with each other and everything else is just a blur, like a disco era cliché. There was no one and nothing in focus but each other. We had never danced for so long without a break before, and never did we do so again. When we finally came home, Jake told me that he was beyond exhausted after working a jewelry counter during Valentine's season, but because he loved me, making me happy and doing everything I wanted was his most important concern. It was the perfect thing to say before we fell asleep in each other's arms, not even caring if icing and scattered candy hearts were still all over my bed.

In all of my long relationship with Jake, our Valentine's date was my happiest memory. Things deteriorated rapidly after a full year together, with both of us to blame. Why we stayed together, I don't know, unless it was because of memories like this, and the hope that we would have them once again. But I will always remember our best date ever, that Valentine's Day when I truly had eyes for no one else but him, and the dream of a love forever seemed, at least in my naive early twenty-something mind, to be something I had finally achieved.

AT PEACE IN THE PINES

GREGORY L. NORRIS

THOUGH IT HAD loomed ominously before us for six weeks on the calendar and bank statements, May 25, 2005 started out much like any other day: roll out of bed, feed the cats, make coffee, shower, and then tackle a seemingly endless plate of obstacles and deadlines. But there was a distinct difference to this date.

I hadn't really slept over the course of the previous night; if anything, I'd simply passed out for breaks of downtime, only to be jolted awake by the scope of what we were about to face. When I'd had enough, I slid out of bed. It was just after dawn on the big day.

The two cats were waiting to be fed: the Tuna Cat, now twenty, who I'd adopted on a snowy December night in my early twenties; and Mesquina, a tiny fifteen-year-old black domestic shorthaired imp who had bonded with my husband Bruce the night he and I met—a pair of penniless romantics too poor to afford what most people would consider a proper first date. Two years earlier almost to the day, we'd rented Guy Pearce's remake of *The Time Machine* and pooled our quarters to buy take-out chicken parmesan sandwiches, flopped in front of the tube, and basked in the joy of getting to know each other. Normally shy Mesquina had stared at the newcomer with enormous, adoring eyes—not my first clue that Bruce was marriage material, but one of the most telling.

I remembered that first date as I roused Bruce from sleep. "It's time to get up," I said, my mouth desiccated of all moisture, the makings of an exquisite headache beginning to pound at my temples. He growled himself awake, a sexy zombie in need of his morning coffee. I slipped into the apartment's claustrophobic pantry and brewed the last pot I would ever make in this place, feeling sick to my stomach.

Taking a shower magnified my building nausea. Loading bags and boxes and essentials into the trunk of the car left me soaked in clammy sweat. Beads of perspiration would continue to pour from my hairline all morning. Hours later, when the business was concluded, I'd realize the deluge for what it was: my body sweating out poison.

"Everything's going to go smoothly," Bruce soothed, dressed in blue jeans and a T-shirt under a sweater, his mending arm recently downgraded to a short cast.

Before we left the apartment, we both showered the cats with pats and kisses. They knew something was afoot—their carriers had come up from our storage cage in the building's cellar and sat just inside the door, telltale signs that something major was soon to come. Something earth-shatteringly life altering, in fact.

. . . . .

A SPACE OF probably no more than two feet separated Bruce and me at the conference table, but after living on raw nerves and a lack of sleep for a week, the distance seemed more like a gulf. I sat quietly with my back to the windows, dripping sweat and choking down my gorge; even so, some unaffected voice in my head reminded me how lucky we were to be in this room on this too-sunny morning. The events of previous years and several recently difficult months for us were being cancelled out with every stroke of the black felt-tipped pens in our hands, past horrors steadily evaporating into nothingness as monstrous stacks of documents flew across the big table, each requiring our signatures.

"And here," the woman would indicate while turning pages. "And here. And just to be safe, here, too."

Bruce reclined in his chair and casually scrawled his blockish signature that's more hieroglyph than penmanship once, twice, sometimes in three places across a single sheet of paper. Sitting tense beside him, my sanity threatening to unspool, anchored only by his presence, I added my sweeping writer's signature next to his, liking the way they looked together side-by-side on the page, one protecting its partner the same way the two of us were doing physically and spiritually for each other from our side of the table.

Remaining on an even keel wasn't as easy for me as I'd anticipated. Normally, I'm the calm one, the brains of the team, you could say. The one who makes things happen and gets the deals done. By this point, any of the thousand or so nightmares that could have derailed us would have already kicked us in the shins had they been given the power to do so, but I just couldn't get my pulse to slow. In addition to being the practical one, I'm a writer, a slave to my imagination. Today, Bruce was the study in coolness, from his baseball cap and the perfect black and silver goatee on his handsome face, his busted left arm, down to his hard athletic butt, which was planted calmly in the seat beside me.

But isn't that how great relationships are supposed to work? When one member of the team falters, the other picks up the slack, moves protectively in front of him to take the bullets and raise him up? Bruce knew without my telling him that, after all the preparation, I was completely out of gas. Every so often, between scrawling his nom-de-glyph in black ink, he would reach his mending left arm across that gulf of twenty-plus inches and pat my leg under the table to reassure me that all would be well, and that the worst was already behind us. Truly, I couldn't have loved him more.

Too much light poured through the room's multitude of floor-to-ceiling windows, the result of a cloudless blue sky—the last day like it we would see for a week. The caustic gourmet coffee I'd been offered upon arrival joined the extra-large cup I'd downed back at the apartment to gnaw steadily at my guts. I vowed never to go through this process again if I could avoid it, convinced that I was seconds away from throwing up everything that was and wasn't in my stomach. But Bruce's touch, and the glances we exchanged over the seemingly endless succession of fresh pages, shepherded me through it.

"We're done," the woman eventually said. "Congratulations. You now own a house."

. . . . .

IT WAS OVER in roughly thirty minutes, half an hour that had felt like an eternity to me. But not to Bruce, I discovered as he started up the car, the key to our new home dangling from the ring in the ignition. For the house he had bought back in that other life B.U.—Before Us—the closing had dragged on for nearly three full hours.

"By comparison, this time was a cakewalk," he said on the drive away from the mortgage company's offices, through Manchester, New Hampshire's circuitous network of roads and highways.

On the loop around the city to the off-ramp that would lead us back to our now ex-apartment to pick up the cats, and from there, north to our sweet little bungalow deep in the pine forests of our adopted new small town, it struck me how vastly different our lives had been less than two years before. The world went out of focus behind a tidal wave of tears, and suddenly, though I couldn't stop crying, the aches at my temples and in my guts abated and I was happier than I could ever recall.

"Do you remember?" I forced out between sips for breath that refused to come easily. "Remember having our coffee on the back steps and the promise we made?"

Bruce reached over and patted my knee. "Of course, sweetie," he said. "We couldn't have done this without all your hard work."

Warm breezes gusted through the car's open windows, smelling less like the city and greener, more like the woods, the longer we traveled away from the downtown. Without warning, the full weight of what we had just accomplished overwhelmed me, a paradox event that turned space and time inside out within the confines of the car. For that sliver of fractured time, we weren't traveling down the interstate, owners of the tiny bungalow built in 1933 that was now our home, but sitting on the back cement steps at the rear entrance to a friend's dilapidated house on a Saturday morning in May of 2003, drinking our morning coffee dressed only in underwear and T-shirts. Bruce was sipping his noxious brew with too much sugar, light on the cream. I nursed mine light, no sugar, from a large cobalt-blue glass mug.

"So tell me what you're looking for," he said.

"Nothing too unreasonable," I answered. "A monogamous relationship. To have a reliable car. To stock up once a month on groceries, so much that you have to squeeze them into that car to make everything fit. To drive home and fill the fridge and cabinets. I went hungry the first summer I worked as a freelance writer. You never forget that."

Of course you didn't—and Bruce hadn't. Summer '03 was a time when we were both strays, like the two cats I'd adopted and for whom he would shortly assume the role of stepdaddy. He'd lost his first house and just about everything else to a bad marriage, and was working for pocket change while sleeping on his employer's sofa in a madhouse of horrors haunted by the central players in said employer's own vicious divorce. I hadn't fared much better after rooming with a former member of a writer's group who was glad to take my half of the rent—in cash—but who hadn't paid any actual rent to the landlord for months. The situation had left me homeless, and only an eleventh-hour solution by a longtime friend from the same group prevented the cats and I from staking out a place beneath the nearest bridge. This friend had relocated to rural Maine; she invited me to crash at her vacant New Englander on the Massachusetts/New Hampshire border for the summer, free of charge apart from paying the utilities. The house sat dirty and neglected, but it was mine until she began extensive renovation plans in the fall so it could be put on the market and sold. This gave me a short window of time to catch my breath and figure out a permanent solution to my housing needs.

I had met Bruce late one night in an Internet chat room, during the transition from one hopeless temporary living situation to another that wasn't much better. Soon after, we met in the real world and had connected on every level that mattered. So completely, our conversations sometimes wandered into that sappy "we were meant to be together" territory.

"And I want something permanent. A home. I want to own a home of my own so I never feel like this again," I said. "You?"

"I want the same things you do, babe. All of them."

The clock was ticking for both of us. I had three months, maybe four, at the New Englander before I would have to move out. Bruce's situation was already tense; unknown to us at the time, just weeks after this discussion it would become utterly chaotic as the ugliness of his employer's divorce reached flashpoint.

"We can do it," I said. "We can buy a house together, I know we can."

Having no money or car were only the first roadblocks preventing the realization of that dream. Accompanying them was a seemingly insurmountable laundry list of jagged peaks: soaring real estate prices, bad credit, and the fact that most of Bruce's furniture and belongings were locked in a backyard shed five states away, deep in New Jersey's agricultural south.

"I'm really good at setting goals and tackling a master plan one step at a time," I said, looking him square in the eye. "I know it sounds like a pipe dream now, but if you want to commit to this, we can make it happen—say, within five year's time? A five-year plan."

Bruce nodded. "I'm with you. Promise."

"I promise, too." We raised our coffee cups, chiming them together. And then we kissed, finished our coffee, and briefly enjoyed the folly of that big, distant dream, never suspecting at the time that it was much closer than either of us dared imagine.

. . . . .

TIME AGAIN FELL onto its normal track of minutes, hours, and days, and I was back in the car with Bruce on May 20, traveling to pick up the cats. From there, we planned to head up to our tiny bungalow situated among the tall pines. I clutched the three folders holding our copies of the documents from the closing in hands that had sweated profusely all morning, enough for my fingertips to absorb the folders' navy color.

"I promised we could do it in five years, but we did it in less than two," I managed. "No more living on friends' couches, or in loud apartments where the air conditioning never works and they refuse to fix it. No more living out of cardboard boxes, feeling like strays. We did it—I'm so proud of us!"

In two short years, we had scaled those jagged peaks one at a time, targeting them without mercy; first in a rented mobile home in a rural corner of our adopted southern New Hampshire town, then in a converted schoolhouse apartment that, lovely as it may have appeared on the outside, proved a loud and cramped existence once we were actually living within its cold, thin walls. Buying a reliable car demanded a bit of a dance on our part. Bruce had landed a new job with benefits at a local company and in record time was scaling the management ladder, but for the better part of 2004, our lack of a vehicle meant he was either walking to work or relying upon friends for a ride. Then in November, thanks to the small bonanza of an unexpected last-minute magazine assignment, I scored a paycheck big enough for a sizeable down payment. We tested one car, knew it was the vehicle we wanted, and waited to be approved for financing.

And waited.

Eventually, stringent conditions were put before us: a bigger down payment and our agreeing to take out an additional power train warranty on the car. I scrambled to come up with the money to meet the terms. At last, in early December, we drove off the lot with the first newer-model car either of us had ever owned.

Months earlier, we had solved the dilemma of moving Bruce's furniture up from Jersey. Over the course of two days, we drove a rental car one-way down, swapped it for a seventeen-foot moving van, backed that up to the shed, then loaded all of Bruce's belongings inside, wiping off cobwebs, spiders, and acorn shells left by the chipmunks that had guarded his possessions during his three-year absence following the end of that other life.

Repairing our credit had been relatively easy, I discovered, after one lone bloodsucking credit card company offered us fifty dollars in credit—all it would cost us was two hundred up front to activate the account. But by choking down my disgust and accepting their terms, by the end of 2004, I had boosted our credit to a decent level—enough, I learned, to land us a low down payment mortgage.

By January 2005, all but one of our mountains had been bested, the biggest one of all: buying a house.

For the previous two years, starting during that terrifying summer when Bruce and I committed to each other while teetering on the edge of homelessness, I got addicted to scrolling through the online real estate listings, sometimes wasting whole days and evenings at the computer feeling lost and sad and downtrodden when I should have been writing. We had almost brokered a deal to buy the mobile home we took when we first moved in together in early September of 2003, but the owners leasing it to us were sleazy, and we never would have owned the land it was set upon. Also, the property was too old to be financed. Unlike conventional real estate, I learned, mobile homes are still classified as vehicles; like automobiles, they go down in value the older they grow, instead of up like traditional homes.

Soon after moving in, the owners put the mobile home on the market, which meant we had to pack up our belongings and move yet again, lugging boxes and furniture down one set of stairs and up another. During that time, the specter of homelessness—along with plenty of hopelessness—bore down upon us once more. We were still chasing a dream, while being chased out of one bad living arrangement into another.

We got the apartment at the town's original schoolhouse. The building, with its massive white columns and bell tower, looked stately on the outside, but the image was illusory. The dishwasher, when it wasn't pouring water all over the floor, would fill with moldy sludge that had backed up through the plumbing. The air conditioner died just in time for a summer heat wave and was never repaired, regardless of numerous calls placed to the landlord. And the walls were so thin, we always knew what our nearest neighbor was watching on his loud widescreen TV.

I scrolled through the real estate listings. Small, sweet homes I would have given anything to own went up on the MLS early in the morning only to come under contract before the end of the same day, thanks to an insane buyer's market the likes of which New England had never before seen. It was vicious out there, especially for a couple of struggling gay men who didn't have much of a down payment or the credit to get financing.

On a gray January morning the first week of 2005, tempted into fantasyland by yet another of those properties teasing me from my computer's screen, I picked up the phone to call the listing agent with a question: might the owner consider financing? The realtor (a youngish woman, I guessed, from her energy) informed me that I should check with a mortgage specialist to see if we had the goods for real financing on a property—in other words, adequate credit. She gave me a number, and I called. And unknown to us, something miraculous had happened by my agreeing to absorb that shitty credit card's terms: I'd boosted our rating to within a handful of the points needed to get us 100 percent financing. A month after that, our credit was good enough to make it happen. Now, we only needed to find our home.

I was blessed as a boy to grow up in a small, enchanted cottage in a woodsy New Hampshire town called Windham. Three decades later, Windham isn't so woodsy or enchanted anymore, but I still return to the town as it was then in the pages of my writing and often in my dreams. That little cottage in the pines set the standards by which Bruce and I would search to find the house of our dreams. We didn't want a "McMansion"—something monstrous constructed of drywall and cheap, non-natural materials. Not that we could have afforded one; we came in at the very bottom of the basement in terms of what we could expect for mortgage financing. Still, we decided the house—if it even existed out there in that merciless, modern day land-grab—would need four important things.

Foremost, it required a minimum of two bedrooms. I'd spent the last year at the schoolhouse writing in the living room, forced to work while our TV (not to mention, the neighbor's) was on. I wanted that second bedroom as a dedicated office space to work in.

It also needed room for a garden. I had gardened throughout my teens and into my early twenties. Once it gets in your blood, gardening is something you must eventually return to, even if the events of your life—like living in an apartment—prevent you from digging in the topsoil, composting, and growing your own food. And growing our own food would help with the grocery bill, I reasoned.

We'd purchased a new washer during our brief stay at the mobile home, but it had sat in the basement of the schoolhouse in our storage cage for a year. So after lugging baskets and bags of laundry to the local laundromat (truly, one of the most depressing places on the planet ever created), we decided any potential house must come with a laundry area.

On a frigid December morning not long before we got approval, a garbage truck cutting short a turn on the main road took out the electrical lines. It would be hours before the power was turned back on, and by that point, the schoolhouse—with its thin walls—had grown unbearably cold. Everything inside the place ran on electricity, so we were unable to work either the stove or the microwave, putting the idea of making a pot of coffee to ward off the chill out of the question. With the horror of that day still fresh in our minds, we demanded our new house also needed to have a backup source of heat, either a fireplace or a woodstove.

And with those four conditions carved in stone, we found our realtor and set out, blissfully unaware of the nightmare ahead of us.

We toured a filthy house set on a full acre that turned out to be owned by the sister of a guy I'd been a friend to in my sophomore year of high school. She didn't remember me, but after I introduced myself, one of her three young daughters slapped me on the ass, telling me I was ugly and fat. One Saturday in February, we put an offer on a chalet-styled fixer-upper that came onto the market the Friday morning before. It was crawling with potential buyers before we even exited our car, and after three weeks of painful waiting, we were told we'd lost the house to a developer who probably had plans to level it anyway. I started to comprehend some of what parents trying to adopt a baby are routinely, mercilessly put through.

We looked at a house in the town of Nottingham, New Hampshire. When I was six, my best friend had moved with his family from Windham to Nottingham. It remains one of the most traumatic turning points of my life—already a bad omen. The house we looked at wasn't much more than four walls held together by mold. The structure had sat unlived in for years and was a total knockdown; anybody buying this property would need to start from scratch. Somebody, however, had kindly placed bowls upside down over the drains in the sink and bathtub. "That's to keep critters from crawling into the house through the plumbing," Bruce said. Then he added that the only things missing to make the picture complete were the blood spatter patterns on the walls and a corpse.

In early March, Bruce slipped on the unpaved parking lot at work during a freak blizzard that shut down the entire state, shattering his left wrist in five places and requiring a long surgery to repair the break (and an even longer period of recovery to regain full use of the arm). The day after the storm, our realtor called about a house that had just gone on the market, and was quite excited to show it to us. I cross-referenced the MLS listing on the computer while forcing food and pain medication on Bruce, and shuddered at the sight of it. It was the *Amityville Horror* set in New Hampshire, but it was in our price range. Bruce insisted on coming along to see it, so I bundled him up and together we hopped into our realtor's truck.

Another realtor was marching a prospective buyer through the house when we got there, and while we had done this dance so many times before, that wasn't what so disheartened me about the place. Before even setting foot inside, I knew I didn't want to live there. The house had no trees. It sat backed up to a busy highway in the shadow of the ridge that the road had been carved out of decades earlier. It would turn out to be the worst of the bunch we saw, a house sold off following a divorce in which the family had fled in the night, literally, with all they could carry. Their bundles didn't involve the fish tank, which had become a block of green ice, with dead fish suspended in hideous poses. They'd shut off the heat when they'd left, dooming their fish. Bad karma pooled in every corner, especially in the sitting room at the rear of the house, where the owner's dogs had broken the windows with their snouts, smearing the glass with blood and saliva before ripping through the screens to escape.

This was no place for us. We left, Bruce in exquisite pain, both of us exhausted and, even worse, convinced we were never going to find our home.

Due mostly to his resolve and a rigorous rehab schedule, Bruce's arm healed ahead of projections, shocking even his orthopedic surgeon. On a Friday night in early April, unable to sleep, I called up the real estate listings and did a search of properties within a twenty-five mile radius of Bruce's job and my writers' group. I followed a link to a small rural town I had never heard of, located right at the outer rim of our search parameters, and very nearly jumped out of my seat.

A small bungalow house set on nearly an acre, with two bedrooms, a wood stove, laundry hookup, antique wide pine floors, and lots of trees had somehow escaped the wrath of the flippers, developers, and other hungry couples seeking their first homes. I called our realtor, and two days later Bruce and I were driving up the interstate. We couldn't get there fast enough.

We entered the neighborhood, wondering at first if we had been given the wrong directions. Most of the places we'd visited to see houses in our price range were the kind you wouldn't walk through after dark—and might worry about walking in during the day. Not so this area; beautiful old homes and lush stretches of green space gently rolled past.

"Are you sure we're in the right place?" he asked.

I counted house numbers as we went up one side of a gently sloping hill and down the other. "I hope so!"

And at the bottom of that hill, we saw the giant boulder set beneath an ancient pine tree with gigantic, sweeping arms, saw the farmer's wall, and the rise of the mostly wooded lot. Sitting at the top of the rise was a small, adorable bungalow set on nearly a full acre, braced against seventy more of conservation land.

Before our realtor met us in the driveway fifteen minutes later, before we'd even set foot inside the house, we knew it was the one we were meant to own. As mysterious as it sounds, the house had spoken to us. This was home.

In the closing, we learned some of the house's history. Built in 1933, it was known around town as "the Bear Camp" because it had once been a summer retreat, and bears were often seen in the morning drinking from the property's small stream. The previous owner, who'd left the place filthy and neglected, was shocked that we planned to keep the small house and renovate it instead of putting up one of those battleship-sized monstrosities like the ones that were going in farther up the road.

During the walk-through with our realtor, I still couldn't allow myself to believe the house would be ours. Something would still go wrong to mess things up. While I emoted, Bruce found more wide pine floors beneath the smelly carpet of the second bedroom, the room that would become my office, and promised that, even with his arm still on the mend, he would tackle sanding and staining them the instant we were moved in so I could get back to my writing work.

A forest of rare lady slipper orchids was in bloom up on the hill at the edge of our tree line. There had been lady slippers growing under the shady pines in the Windham of my boyhood. The Bear Camp's little stream serenaded us with its babble.

No, we couldn't even hope to dream that by the end of the day, this would all be ours.

But it was.

. . . . .

BY NOON, OUR two cats were yowling a symphony from their carriers in the back seat of the car. The road took that familiar dip toward the big boulder and the towering pine, and suddenly, there rose the little bungalow before us.

We lugged in the cat carriers and freed our little brood. Slinking with their shoulders hunched and their bellies low to the ground, Tuna and Mesquina checked out the house. Part of me realized I was walking around in the same manner as the cats, too nervous to believe we had arrived in a permanent place of our own.

"This is your home now, and for forever," Bruce said to the cats. Then he turned to me. "And ours, too, honey."

We embraced. It *was* real. We had made it so.

"This is the one of the two best days of my life," I told him.

"What's the other?"

"The day I met you."

TRAVELS
TOGETHER

WE'LL ALWAYS HAVE PARIS

BOB ANGELL

BEN AND I met in October of 1988, when he was a junior at George-town University and I was an engineer with a defense contractor and nine years out of college. He was two inches taller than me, and had the grace of the young. I was a triathlete, built for endurance and not for display. He was an introvert, and I was at home in a crowd. He came out in high school; I was still having problems with it.

That first Christmas break he came back to campus a week early to be with me. He didn't go to his folks for spring break, and we went to Florida instead. That summer he took an internship in D.C. that turned into a part-time job. We used to joke that we were lesbians because he moved in right away, we spent all our time together, and we liked it that way.

We were both towheads as kids, hair white as snow with the complexions that go with it. Though our hair darkened with age, we still burn easily from the sun, not to mention from the wrong glance or word—high potential for a little drama. We fought like cats and dogs. My friends gave it six months, then made a habit of recasting their bets.

Ben had already completed his language proficiency requirement his sophomore year; he'd taken AP French in high school and had been an American Field Service exchange student. A summer in France with a family on a farm in the Loire Valley had helped make him nearly fluent. Ben liked languages and he was taking German. I had always wanted to learn French (I took Spanish in high school) so I began taking night classes to give me something to do while he was studying. I had this secret dream that we would speak French at home and sometimes out in public, and I imagined wine and cheese and a life of society and romance.

By the time he was to graduate he'd taken two years of German and I'd had a year and a half of French under my belt. Ben landed a job at the agency where he worked. He had also been accepted into a German-language immersion program in Trier, Germany through his university, and he negotiated an end-of-summer start at the new job so he could go.

Airfare to Europe back then was expensive, something about fuel prices and so on, but any price looked like extortion to someone on a student's budget. He thought about not going. What would it matter in the long run anyway? We moped around, agonizing over the decision: he for the cost of it, and I for the selfish reason that I would miss him. He would be gone for over two months, longer than we had ever been apart.

Graduation was hurtling toward us, and the time to commit was at hand. He had to go to Germany; it was a once in a lifetime opportunity. He had done so much for me: brightened my life, challenged the hell out of me, made me happy and content and at ease in the world. So one night, at the El Torito restaurant over a pitcher of sangria, I proposed.

This was the proposition: I had frequent flyer miles enough for two round-trip tickets to Paris; why not go to France together for a week or so, and then he could take a train to Trier and I could spend a week running around France?

Voila!

To sweeten the deal, Ben's brother lived in Paris, and we could stay there as long as we liked for free.

. . . . .

CHRISTOPHE'S APARTMENT WAS on *le quatrième étage*, which literally means fourth level, but is really the top floor in a five-story walkup. The nomenclature is a little French quirk to disguise the fact that you are farther from ground level than it sounds, possibly making it easier to rent such a tiny studio apartment, or make it psychologically easier to climb all those stairs. At any rate, it was a classic Parisian building with a slate Mansard roof, and the window served up breathtaking hints of Paris through a canopy of chestnut trees. Saint Denis, as the tortoiseshell *plan de Paris* shows, is in the tenth *arrondissement*; not a bad place, and very convenient.

Christophe was quite the nerd, an engineer with an aeronautical firm, and not your typical rail-thin Parisian. But he did dress all in black and followed new-wave music and alternative culture with a vengeance. He had all he needed: a roughly eight-by-eight room with a petite sink, a standard college-sized refrigerator, and a front-to-back two-burner stovetop with the smallest oven I'd ever seen underneath. The walls had long ago been painted cream, the trim white. There wasn't a single piece of art; Christophe said it made the place look bigger, but you could see shadows where things had once hung, and the painted nails that held them studded the walls.

There was a closet to the right of the door and a miniature bathroom to the left that would make a sailboat proud: a shower stall you couldn't bend over in (we won't go there), a sink the size of a large coffee cup, and a low-flow toilet that sucked its contents out with such force that it would be terrifying and dangerous for a guy to remain seated while flushing.

Outside his door and across the hall was a *pissoir*, essentially a closet with a hole in the floor near the back with places for your feet should you need to squat over it. Next to that was the stairwell, a shaft of air defined by a gracefully curving staircase that terminated on a black-and-white checkered floor five stories below.

The surrounding neighborhood was nice, convenient with a *boulangerie*, a *patisserie*, a *charcuterie*, a few bistros, and the Saint Denis Métro stop—our gateway to all of Paris. There was plenty to do, what with the museums, *jardins*, *rue du* this and that, and the cafés and late-night bistros to explore. We occupied ourselves during the day while Christophe was at work, and he entertained us well at night.

It was oddly affirming to be in a place where an American queer can't tell if the men are gay or just European. More than that, it was downright liberating. Not that Ben and I have ever been ones to hold hands in public. Even today, we gay men grow up trained away from such displays, in part because there are no role models doing it, and in part because society sanctions the teasing, taunting, and beating of it out of you by your peers in school, and more subtly in the later courses of life. We are like pigeon chicks when it comes to love, PDA, etcetera—affection is always somewhere out of sight, so you don't see teenaged boys lying around on the beach or in parks smooching with each other, and that's a shame.

Without warning, it dawned on us that we had one last full night together. The next night, we would turn in early and then Ben would be whisked away from the Gare de l'Est for Trier the following morning. There were tons of things we had yet to do, like crack open the guide to gay Paris. Christophe had gone to work, and as was usual we had crawled into his bed to snooze on something more comfortable than a thin rug and borrowed sleeping bags.

We awoke curled together in boxers and T-shirts with June sunlight streaming through the window. I opened my eyes and shifted my head back so I could see all of his face. His eyes were wide and staring off at the ceiling.

"You okay?"

"I leave day after tomorrow," he said, and held my arm across his chest.

There is a reason one of his close friends calls him Bendrama. But he hit my panic button with that one. We were at once the condemned, with one full day to live. His touch was suddenly electric, his skin impossibly warm and smooth, and his lips found mine, my fingers glided into his soft, golden hair. We had been somewhat restrained since arriving (we weren't sure Christophe really understood about our relationship, and we hadn't come out and said the words *nous sommes pédés*) but all that was forgotten; the place was ours in that moment, and the walls shook with us.

We tidied up and took the Métro to the Beaubourg where we found a shaded table at some sidewalk café next to the fountain of fantasy machines; a huge rectangular pond about a tenth of an acre in size, across which were scattered things like giant red lips spitting water, a musical G-clef, wheels, rainbow-painted spirals, a rainbow sun god thing with outstretched arms, and an odd little blue hat. Most of the things were motorized, and all spit or showered water over the surface, with an ivy-covered wall on one side and an ancient cathedral on the other for backdrops.

Sparrows flitted in the branches above us and hopped under round café tables or skirted the legs of the French-twist chairs with backs shaped like wrought-iron hearts. There was a big red heart sculpture in the fountain, and I pointed it out.

"There, behind the roving lips." I pulled my chair closer so we could touch knees if we wanted. "You can think of my heart waiting for you across the water when you pass through here again."

He shifted in his chair. "Ouch!"

I'd gotten him with my knee. "Sorry," I said.

Okay, I made that up. Maybe. I'm not sure. But we did get that table by that fountain, near those lips and that red, red heart, and we had our *café au lait* and croissants with chocolate. Without thinking, he'd reach over and wipe a smear of chocolate from my lips, or I his. We nibbled the morning away oblivious of the performers in the plaza. On our walking tour through the narrow shop-lined streets or the *parfumeries* on the Champs d'Elysées, our hands would briefly find a shoulder, or a back, and we'd bump into each other on purpose and laugh.

Sidewalk *crêpes* with Nutella? Sure. Pizza with an egg on it?

Very French. A hamburger *avec salade*? Yes, but of course put the lettuce and tomato on our buns. We grinned at the innuendos and ordered *pommes frites* to go with them. Everything was sexual, everything sexy: the way his blue striped T-shirt draped across his shoulder, tucked into his jeans; the way they rode across his butt and tightened around his strong soccer thighs as he walked.

We critiqued the Habitrail-like escalators and colorful pipes, water mains, and ducting that covered the exterior of the Centre Pompidou, then went inside to see his favorite Van Gogh painting, *The Church at Auvergne*. I bought him a poster of it in the gift shop, which I would lose on the flight home. But I didn't know that yet, like I didn't know what two months of sleeping alone would be like or whether, in his two months of German immersion with a pack of other students, he would find other lips and other hearts. All I knew for sure was that we were in love now, we were here now, and that it would be unbearable to live without him.

We went back to the apartment to get ready for the night. We were going to dinner, and then on to check out gay Paris. I copied a list of bars from the Damron's guide that Ben would take to Germany. Christophe arrived from work, interrupting a little smooch fest, and probably catching us red-faced and giggling. We drank a bottle of wine with him and talked about going out to dinner and so forth alone.

"Ah, this is a good list," Christophe said after snatching my piece of paper. He pulled out a pencil. "*Oui. Oui.* No!" he exclaimed, scratching out a bar. "Ah yes. You must go here," he insisted, adding a name to the list and handing it over. "Everyone goes to *Le Boy*."

I seem to remember that Christophe also gave us the name of a very trendy restaurant, even got us reservations. The restaurant, whose name eludes me, was down some narrow cobblestone street lined on each side with stone-faced storefronts with apartments upstairs, and like everywhere you went in Paris, cats looked down at you from the balconies and windows above.

The trendy restaurant was underground. We wound our way singly down a narrow spiral staircase into what was probably an old wine cellar, or made to look like one. They had fake archways in the walls, and pots of hanging plants acted somewhat as room dividers. Very chic. The patrons were beautiful, of course, perfectly dressed and accessorized, mostly staring into each other's eyes, sipping red wine and nibbling on baguettes and gobs of cheese arrayed on boards with little identifying flags stuck into them.

Everyone was on the appetizer course. That was fine with us. We did what the natives were doing and stared into each other's eyes across our little table for two. We'd barely looked at the wine list before the waiter glided over to take our orders. We'll have this wine, and salads for starters. Just the house salad, please.

"No, *monsieur*," the waiter said, and tapped our menus. "I will return."

He was funny. We laughed. We looked at our menus. They served cheese: cheese appetizers; boards of cheeses entirely from particular countries; combinations of similar and dissimilar cheese tastes and textures for main courses; and cheeses for dessert; sweet cheeses, salty cheeses. These were not offerings made with cheese, like baked brie, cheese omelets, pizza, or cheesecake. No. These were offerings of cheese. That's it. Nothing else. Nada. Not a bit of fiber anywhere, if you excluded the plants hanging around us.

"What do you want to do?" I asked, leaning across the table after moving the candle out of our way.

"I kind of want a salad, now," Ben said. "You want what you can't have."

"You can have it if you really want it." That innuendo again. We liked it here.

"I want it."

The waiter glided over bearing wine, and made a big deal out of it. I wanted to hold the cork in my mouth and pass it to Ben's lips for show. The motif of the day had me in its grip.

"And for dinner, gentlemen?"

"My boyfriend here would like a salad," I said, in a tasteful but loud American voice. Remember, we had already been drinking.

'I'm sorry, *monsieur*—"

"Can't your cook *cook*?" I looked around at the cheese boards and the eyes that glanced our way, and glossed over the fact that salads weren't cooked either. My English was perfect, and I'm certain everyone understood me. "My boyfriend and I would like a salad, please." I felt like a knight on a white horse at that point; I'd do anything for Ben and I wasn't afraid to let everyone know it. Damn it.

We sent *garçon* off to ask the chef, and sat there grinning at each other and drinking *vin rouge*. I can only imagine what they thought of us; Americans! Queers! American queers! We'd seen fliers all over the place that afternoon titled "Act Up—Paris" for a protest about something Jacques Chirac did on *le 7 juin dernier*. I have one of them tucked away in my photo album, which is why I remember it. Perhaps they were afraid we were *homosexuels radicals* and would start a kiss-in on the staircase and block the exit?

Whatever they thought, we got our salads; they handed them over like keys to the city. Paris now belonged to us and the night was young, not quite midnight.

Next stop: Subway, a smoky bar down a dirty cobblestone alley whose front was somehow open to the night and neon. Club music wrapped us in our universal culture. They had pool tables in the back, and guys in leather chaps standing around in the front. We ordered beer. Everyone was drinking Budweiser, so that's what we drank. They liked Americans there. We leaned against the bar and glued ourselves together for a while, cleaning the salad greens off each other's teeth.

This guy in jeans, a leather vest, and a cap appeared right in front of me and stared me in the face. He was only about a foot away; they have different ideas about personal space in France.

"I think he wants you," Ben said in my ear.

"Hello," I said, my arms still around Ben.

The guy said nothing, did nothing, just stared.

"Yep. He wants you."

"Sorry," I said. "I'm taken. Thanks anyway."

The guy didn't budge.

"Shoo. Go away."

"Don't be rude."

"I don't want him," I said, and turned to Ben. The guy was gone when next we looked up.

And then we were at *Le Boy*, a warehouse-looking place from the outside, and a line of glittering people stretched down the velvet-roped block and around the corner. I followed Ben on this one; he was the expert. I had tagged along with his friends to some of the trendiest places in D.C., and it was all about attitude and how many alcohol fortifications you'd had on approach.

We walked right up and right on in. When the bouncer taking cover charges said, "*Excuse-moi*," Ben flipped his hand up like waving off a mosquito. In we went. The city truly was ours for the taking.

It was dark inside, palatial, with black-fabric draped walls, disco balls, lasers in red, green, blue that swept overhead to the perfect music, and it went on and on. A metal staircase led up to a balcony that ran down the long wall in the grand room, opposite a long bar on which boys in jockstraps and bowler hats danced and never kicked a drink. There were glittering boa-waving drag queens flowing through the room.

I bought our first round of hundred-franc-a-piece beers, about twenty bucks. What the hell. We had another round and danced until we were soaked in sweat, then took beers up on the balcony and made out like teenagers. If I were to say things were a little hazy at that point, I'd be right and I'd be wrong. I remember I dropped a thousand francs on beer that night and that we had a fabulous time. I don't remember the tunes they played, or much else about *Le Boy*, except that Ben was the best looking guy in the world and he was all mine and there was nothing we couldn't do together.

Except maybe get back to Christophe's.

We stumbled out into the diffuse gray light of dawn that sucked the sequins off the night and spat them curbside. A cab rolled by trolling for passengers and we took the bait and climbed in. It was a beautiful little cab, with velour interior and very comfortable seats, and I hugged Ben to my chest and watched the empty streets go by.

The cabbie dropped us at the Saint Denis Métro stop since I couldn't remember the exact address. The McDonald's (yes, I know) was open on the far side of the weird intersection where too many streets came together, so we went over there and got hamburgers and fries to go. *Avec la salade.*

All I remember is that on the way back, Ben sat down hard on an alley curb. The tarmac looked stretched there, and ancient cobblestones were working their way to the surface. He threw up, and I held him and made sure he didn't get any of it on his clothes. The napkins came in handy, and the large cokes were a blessing. We sat there for a while, until the sunbeams showered down the street to glitter in the dewy chestnut leaves, and the little cars of Paris started rolling by on their way to work.

We used the *pissoir* together, crossing streams and giggling like kids, then let ourselves into Christophe's apartment to find him freshly showered and leaving for work. Then he was gone, and we brushed our teeth and tumbled together into bed for the grand finale.

Perfect.

At the Gare de l'Est, we stood on the platform, his duffle bags at our feet, holding each other. I'm certain steam billowed out from under the train just like in the movies, and uniformed conductors with flattop caps threaded through the rush of passengers, directing them to their proper cars.

"I don't want to go," Ben said, nuzzling closer.

"I don't want you to go." I held on, the tightness in my throat forced me to swallow, my eyes to water.

"I'm scared."

I knew exactly what he was saying. He was going alone to an unknown place where there were unfamiliar people, stern people in an unfamiliar country, with foreign students he didn't know. He didn't know if he would like any of them.

And what if he *did* find one he liked?

"I'm scared, too." I hugged him tight through his waterproof jacket, hoping if I cried that some of the tears would stain his shirt. Permanently.

"I'm going home with you," he said. "They'll refund most of it."

"I would love it if you came home with me." It was what I wanted more than anything. "But you'll be fine. I know it. You'll be home in no time, and dreaming in German. I'll need an interpreter when you talk in your sleep."

"What about you?"

I hugged him tighter, and yeah, tears were dropping. Damned allergies. "I'll be waiting for you."

And yes we kissed, right there in front of everyone.

META-ANALYSIS OF THE EFFECTS OF LOVE ON TOFU

BARRY LOWE

"**BUT WHY WOULD** they name a town after the past tense of a verb?" The little voice came from the plane seat next to me. Wally, who was a seat farther over, ignored the question and squeezed closer to the window as if he didn't know me or our little baby dinosaur strapped in the seat between us who had asked the, in my estimation, quite reasonable question.

We'd hit Bled in northwestern Slovenia because Wally had returned home, a few months earlier, from his fifty-eighth straight week of overtime and exploded, "I can't take it any more!!!!!!!!!!!!!!!" The line of exclamation marks does not signify semantic laziness, rather an attempt to express, rather poorly in print, the combination of explosive emphasis on "more" and the grinding of teeth.

After thirty-five years of systematically pepping up our relationship with drugs, alcohol, adultery, acupuncture, Atkins, group sex, pornography, chiropractic and ESP therapy, in no particular order or combination, we were after a bit of alone time. Time away from friends, acquaintances, utility bills, being locked into cable television schedules and the constant anxiety of the new millennium, not to mention having to douche every Friday night for those sudden unexpected visitors who would crawl round for a quickie after their girlfriends had closed the vaginal gate.

In a sudden pique of consideration for his care of me during

my convalescence from being surgically rendered an almost obso-
lete form of punctuation, a semicolon, from my tussle with cancer,
I allowed him to choose the destination that most appealed to
him. He'd worried and cajoled me through chemotherapy and a
stomach wound so stubborn it spat parsley and soy sauce if I so
much as laughed.

"I'd like to go home," he said without having to think about
it, immediately pricking my romantic notions of trekking the Hi-
malayas in Bhutan or snuggling up with a cute Mongolian in his
yurt.

And home did not mean our heavily mortgaged inner city
apartment, but rather Malta, a tiny lint speck in the Mediterra-
nean dislodged from the boot of Italy, from whence Wally had
migrated with his family fifty years before at the age of five, and to
which he had not, as yet, returned. And as an added tease to make
the anticipation of "going home" that much sweeter, we decided
to make our approach leisurely—by way of Italy.

We were to be accompanied on our travels by our lucky mas-
cot, a tiny, intractable, opinionated baby dinosaur named Tofu.
The more psychobabbly inclined of our friends put our adoption
of said creature down to my frustrated paternal desire, instead of
to the fact that I can ventriloquize the most childish and sarcastic
aspects of my personality into the little "stuffed toy" as our more
dismissive friends denigrate him. I do have to admit Wally's love
for our adoptee is considerably less than mine and he has threatened on numerous occasions to bin the "animal", but on the one
occasion he attempted it, I didn't speak to him for a week. Never,
but never, cross an obsessive compulsive.

When Tofu heard we were heading off on an overseas adventure, he read every highly illustrated guide book my credit card
could afford (you will just have to accept him as a living entity or stop reading now) and made one request. Well, he made
hundreds, being the selfish little shit he is, but this one was, at
least, poignant. It stemmed from an occasion when he had been
propped up in front of the television with his own remote control

and he'd come across a movie version of *Pinocchio*. From that moment, his abiding passion had been to become human. Wally and I knew it was a fantasy (yes, we can discern fantasy from reality even though it may not seem like it), but Tofu had read that a teardrop shaped island, Blejski Otok, an added touch of perfection on Bled's postcard-perfect alpine lake, was home to a baroque church, the Church of the Assumption, which houses a fifteenth-century magic bell. The legend is that it grants a wish to anyone making it peal from their first tug on the rope. Tofu believed, in the depths of his little plastic heart, that he would ring that bell and become a real little boy, or actually, a real little boy dinosaur.

We couldn't deny him, and anyway, the flight was cheaper into Slovenia than it was into Italy.

His excitement on the hand-propelled gondola ride over to the island was matched only by his eagerness to scale the arduous South Staircase, with scant regard for the historical architectural niceties along the way, and barrel his way to the belfry. Being only eight inches tall, Tofu, of course, needed my help. The other tourists in the chapel were most amused that a tiny dinosaur was attempting to ring the bell that they'd already failed miserably to clang.

So, with his little hands (do dinosaurs have hands?) gripped in mine and Wally attempting to chameleon himself into the woodwork of the pews in embarrassment, we gave the bell rope one almighty tug and waited for the Almighty to do his thing. The silence was painful. "Pull it again," someone called, but we both knew if it didn't ring the first time the wish was void. Then, just a whisper of a strike before the bell pealed high up in the tower, and Tofu's little plastic face lit up with excitement at the metamorphosis to come. But it didn't. And by the time we'd reached the lake shore on the return gondola, he realized he was still nothing more than a plastic replica of a television sitcom character. And one whose series had been canceled over a decade before.

"Maybe it's because you're not a Catholic," Wally suggested, to prevent Tofu from becoming too depressed. "Or maybe the Lake

Bled god doesn't like dinosaurs. Especially gay dinosaurs."

"Why do you want to be human anyway?" I asked. "You just get to feel lots of pain and misery and disappointment. Just like now."

"You just think I feel those things," he said. "They're just words I've heard on television. But I don't feel them. And I want to feel that one everybody goes gooey over and talks about all the time."

"What one's that?" Wally asked.

"Love."

That night I distinctly heard muffled snufflings from the drawer in which he was sleeping, and the handkerchief he'd used for a pillow was decidedly damp the next morning.

"I know," I said. "Let's go see the Pope. We're going to Rome anyway so we'll drop in and see if he can grant your wish. After all, this is his church."

"Maybe the warranty has run out?" Tofu suggested hopefully.

We had one more stop before we left town. It was by way of a pilgrimage to the small café, Slaščičarna Šmon, near the bus station, awash with a sea of yellow custard and flaky pastry. Being of an inquisitive culinary disposition, especially of the cream kind, we had heard rumors that *kremna rezina*, created in the town in the 1950s, was a source of national pride.

"But it's just a plain old vanilla slice," Wally complained when he first saw it. He couldn't keep the disappointment out of his voice when it was brought to our table, and he proceeded to prod it with his fork as if it were some alien custard life form.

"Mmph, wait till you taste it," I said as I hoed into more of it. It may have been plain old vanilla slice back home in Sydney but here it was like biting into a small pocket of vanilla-flavored cloud. It melted in the mouth like custard cotton candy. No wonder it was considered a national treasure.

"Oh—My—God!" Wally said as he scooped it into his mouth. "It really was worth coming all this way for it."

We were hooked, and so good were they we bought another four as take-aways for our long bus ride, although Tofu turned his nose up at having to share rather crowded quarters, my backpack, with a plate of wobbling custard cream and flaky pastry. "I'm all covered in icing sugar," he complained, and sneezed impolitely to emphasize his annoyance.

By the time we got to Rome the *kremna rezina* were gone and so was the Pope. As a consolation, we took Tofu to the Vatican Museum where he got a crick in his neck from admiring the ceiling. "Why would anyone in their right mind paint anything way up there? You need a stepladder to see it properly." His unfulfilled close encounter of the papal kind was assuaged by the Sistine Chapel souvenir coloring book we bought for him at the Vatican shop, as he just knew he could show Michelangelo a thing or two when it came to color. "It needs lots more red. And if you add a few dicks it'll have queens flocking to see it. Don't the Pope's men know anything about marketing?" Tofu asked in his wide-eyed, no eyelids sort of way. "And what's with all the gold plates around everybody's head in the paintings?"

"It symbolizes that person is a saint," Wally explained as patiently as anyone could to a piece of molded plastic. Wally was embarrassed by Tofu's public pronouncements, but was highly amused by his private opinions.

"What's a saint?"

"A saint is a special person who performs miracles."

"Like turning plastic dinosaurs into living, feeling creatures?"

"Uh huh."

"So what you're telling me is all I need is a gold plate stuck to the back of my head and then I can perform a miracle and make myself feel love?" he said with commendable common sense.

"Um, I think the miracles have to come first," Wally said.

We could see his little hollow head was attempting to think it over as we placed him in the hotel drawer for safekeeping during the night.

"He won't give up," I said. "But I have an idea that might please him."

The next day we headed for Malta. Wally's greatest fear was

that I would use the smattering of Maltese curses I had picked up over the years on one of the custom's officials, or that Tofu would let fly with his favorite Maltese expletive which roughly translates as "dick breath" if one of said officials should prod him to see if he contained drugs. "I don't have even a rudimentary anal canal so how could I conceal drugs?" Tofu said when I warned him.

My fear was that Wally would find his homeland a disappointment.

Wally was keeping his emotions in check on the short plane flight, which was all to the good as Tofu was, as usual, causing a ruckus. He hated it when a plane was at capacity and he was assigned an uncomfortable berth in the magazine rack at the back of the seat in front. He would sit in what he called the "string bag" and glare for the entire trip. Or until he forgot his funk.

"How can I be a saint? The plate's not gold. It's white and it's made of plastic," he grizzled.

"How ungrateful can you be?" I remonstrated.

"And it smells of pastries. I bet real saints don't smell like a bakery."

"It's the best we could do on the spur of the moment," I said.

"You're so cheap. I bet this is the plate left over from the take-away vanilla slices you bought and thought I wouldn't notice."

He was right of course.

"And I bet the Pope didn't bless it at all."

I had told him a small lie to placate him and keep his hopes alive. I shook my head.

"Well, fuck the Pope," Tofu said.

Wally gave me a withering look.

"I'm going to start my own religion. I hereby declare myself a saint. And to show my purity I have a white plastic halo. And no mention please that it's plastic."

"If you're a saint," Wally said, "you need to be Saint somebody or the other."

"Open the map of Malta," Tofu said, and putting one arm over his eyes his little hand poked the map. "There, that's my name.

Saint um Bugger er Saint Buggybar."

"It's pronounced Boo-jee-ba," Wally smiled.

"Okay, so I'm Saint Buggiba. That sounds good."

He fell asleep while calculating all the ways he could bilk money from what he hoped would be his considerable future congregation, and got his foot tangled in the crocheted seat pocket when we landed.

We sailed through customs uneventfully, Wally flashing his Maltese passport for the first time in the twenty years he'd had one, and me managing to keep my tongue in check as Tofu, all sweetness and piety, protruded from my backpack, his head and his outstretched arms beseeching all and sundry to worship him, or at least come along for a hug.

Wally was emotionally raw, so Tofu and I backed off and gave him time to acclimatize himself to the womb of his formative years. We unpacked in silence at our self-contained apartment until Tofu discovered that, from our third-floor balcony, we could see straight into the dormitories and showers of the backpackers' hostel opposite. As it was the height of summer, all the windows were wide open, revealing male and female backpackers who had the modesty of a *Playgirl* centerfold.

"You chose the accommodation well," Wally smiled.

"It wasn't deliberate. I had no idea."

And his few remaining relatives on the island had no idea he had returned. The family bond remains tight among the Maltese and their expatriate kinfolk. We'd learned from expat friends that once they know you're "coming home," they turn up at the airport and ferry you from one relative to another, and all you see of the country is the inside of people's residences spruced up for the occasion and whatever vistas can be readily viewed from a car window. We did, however, have one date lined up: with Wally's aunt, his mother's sister, who still lived in the same house she did when Wally and his family had left for Australia in the 1950's.

The date was for dinner at her house on the very last night of our stay, that way no one could monopolize our time. We were free in the intervening week to wander the seafront for our after-noon "parmigiano" as Tofu called it, sitting at the waterfront cafés of Sliema nibbling on pastizzi, or taking a dip in the Mediter-ranean with locals of all ages, who didn't give my portly scarred body a second glance, even in disgust, unlike the slim lithe gay youngsters at Bondi. We strolled through the old sandstone capi-tal of Valetta and explored the megalithic temples at Tarxien, and the walled city of Mdina. And best of all, we relaxed and snuggled and snogged, as Wally's apprehensiveness relaxed into joy. He had found his birth home, for all its annoyances, a most welcoming place.

We ignored the newspapers, there was no television in our self-contained apartment, and the tension oozed out of our bod-ies along with the perspiration. We sipped wine on the balcony and watched the young backpackers across the street, or listened to the young men on the balcony below ours, luxuriating semi-na-ked with their pick-ups of the previous night until their smoking drove us indoors.

And then, the all-too-soon dinner date with the aunt who lived in Marsaxlokk. "Oooh," Tofu had squealed when he heard our des-tination. "I love all those Maltese names with the unpronounce-able x's and q's. No one back home will know how to pronounce them, so I hereby declare myself St. Bugibba or Marsaxlokk." Ad-mittedly, it took him three or four attempts to wrap his little plas-tic tongue around the correct pronunciation.

"You're not taking him," Wally said, horrified at the thought.

"You're certainly not going without me," Tofu huffed.

We compromised, and Tofu was tucked into my backpack as we made for the bus, the only evidence of his existence the muffled cries of "Let me out! Let me out!" until he came up for air once aboard and was suitably impressed that the driver had turned his cabin area into a mini shrine replete with crucifix, a small font of holy water, and numerous colored likenesses of some patron saint or other, all of which featured the ubiquitous golden halo. Tofu made a quick Post-it note reminder to get some 3-D postcards of himself in official robes with his plastic plate on our return to Australia.

It wasn't difficult to find his aunt's maisonette after the bus dropped us off. Wally's childhood homing beacon kicked in but he became more nervous as we got closer. He hung back until I marched up to the door and rang the bell. After a second buzz a head popped over the upstairs balcony, followed by a shriek of recognition—although there had been a split-second quizzical registration of the strange man with eyebrow rings and earrings carrying a plastic dinosaur beside the prodigal nephew.

It was a whirling dervish of reminiscences and introductions. I sat outside the eye of the nostalgia as Wally was examined, like a foreign insect under the microscope of cultural differences, and I was examined peripherally in an effort to determine my position in the pantheon. The conversation broke from English into Maltese and back again with the regularity of an English train timetable. Aunt and uncle and their assorted adult children, who had assembled for the occasion, showered Wally with family news and gossip, and showed us from their kitchen window the house down the street where Wally's father had shouted the news of his birth to the relatives and the neighborhood.

There was the inevitable cramming of fifty years into four hours, and the niggling distrust of a returning expatriate by the generations who remained behind, especially as Wally's brother, Joe, was also visiting his homeland, with his girlfriend to whom he was unwed. It had fallen to poor "fallen" Joe to explain Wally's and my marital (or lack thereof) situation. The response had been shock, followed by stoic resignation and the aunt's, "I never would have believed it. He's the last one in the family I would have expected it of. When he was born he had the most perfect little tool."

So, the cacophonous outpouring of affection and pleasure, tinged with a soupçon of disapproval, continued throughout the meal, until we all retired to the third floor roof space. It was the feast day of the church that the house overlooked and the locals were crowding the streets, even though it was late, in preparation for the fireworks. Children were pushing molded chairs along the sidewalk in a game they had invented to relieve the boredom, causing much consternation in Tofu who shuddered at the thought of fragile plastic scraping along concrete. The adults, ignoring them, drank as they played cards in the streets or sat in the gutters with their neighbors.

On the rooftop, well lubricated by the wine, we watched the late-night fireworks over the church, and for a moment could appreciate the comfort of faith without capitulating to its abrogation of personal responsibility to the almighty powerful super being. We'd attempted to discuss it in the past with Tofu, whose response had been a simple "Well, if you don't give me what I want I'll destroy you."

The fireworks bruised the sky with their haphazard slaps of gaudy color until our group began to wander back down to the maisonette's living room for coffee. Wally and I lingered, and I propped Tofu on the edge of the roof parapet.

"Oooh," Tofu said in awe, and he clapped his little hands at the last spurts of explosive celebration that turned the night sky blue and pink and green. "Is this all for me?"

I held Wally's hand and leaned over and kissed him.

Tofu, confused for a moment, his heart racing at the excitement of his first live fireworks display and the sheer exuberance of a new life experience, reached out for our hands, and as the three of us stood and watched the giant dome in its final paroxysm of illumination, asked dreamily, "Is this what love is? Dazzling colored lights, big explosions, being with people you really like?"

"Close enough," I said.

EMBRACING LIFE

D.J. IRELAND

MONTE TESTACCIO, LEGEND has it, began life in ancient times as a pile of discarded *amphorae*, a Roman dumping ground, and derives its name from *testae*, the Latin for potsherds. It is either ironic or appropriate, depending on your point of view, that it now forms a focus for some of the more alternative forms of Rome's peculiar nightlife. Around midnight, particularly on Fridays and Saturdays, the streets in the area fill up with a stream of small cars, taxis, and couples on foot, all heading in the same direction, turning onto a road that seemingly leads to nowhere.

The road is lined at first with stylish restaurants; then with small, increasingly dark, cellar bars; and finally—at a kind of opening out into a dusty, ramshackle turning place—it becomes a surreal market square of larger clubs, some of general interest, others seeming to cater to more mysterious and arcane specialties. The traffic flow continues beyond this *agora* down two dark, dangerous alleyways which appear to lead only toward rubbish heaps and junkyards, but in reality serve as single-file car parks, impromptu *pissoirs*, and—toward dawn, but before sunrise—as cruising grounds for a brutal and inelegant version of the traditional *passeggiata*.

It was down this long road, toward this surreal film set of a place, that we had cautiously made our way earlier that evening. Now we are sitting somewhat awkwardly, side-by-side, at a table in a small club called Testaccolo. Awkwardly not because of any discomfort with each other, but because our heads bump into a shelf which runs along the wall. Presumably it had been designed to be a convenient waist height for standing against and placing drinks on, but someone had arranged a row of small marble tables and wrought iron chairs immediately beneath it, thus denying both the shelf's purpose and the comfort of anyone sitting beside or beneath it.

I'm musing over the name of the club, trying to decide whether the implication—to an Englishman—of testicles is intentional, or whether it's an innocent variation on Testaccio. Despairing at my weak grasp of the Italian language, my thoughts turn to Norwegian and the fact that my companion chooses to pronounce his name more like Life, though not exactly, and less like the Layf I would have expected. He is staring into space, thinking, his head gently swaying to the beat of the music, the loudness of which has made any conversation impractical.

I focus on the crowd around us now, and amuse myself by watching to see which of them are openly fascinated by Leif's extreme blond hair and blue-eyed Nordic looks. That morning, I had laughed—perhaps rather too enthusiastically—when a black-haired, fallen angel of a *ragazzo* had passed us outside the Pantheon, caught sight of Leif, and had been so captivated that he'd walked straight into an elegant young woman traveling in the opposite direction.

I'm sure she was torn whether to be more annoyed at being bumped into or by the fact that the youth had been eyeing up my companion and not her. Leif had not been so amused, and had hinted that he felt I was a little too aware of who was looking at whom and for what purposes . . .

. . . . .

THIS EVENING, WE HAD stopped to eat at a scruffy *trattoria* in a side street near our Trastevere hotel. Had we been more patient or braver, and waited until we had reached Testaccio itself, we would probably have found somewhere more stylish. Instead, we were shown into a small, stuffy room, with three lino-covered tables and some religious prints of rather dubious taste. The waiter spoke to us in bad English. I replied in even worse Italian, which prompted him to apologize for his English; I felt guilty for the unintentional insult. A sense of awkwardness—dislocation—continued in our conversation as we waited for the food. We had somehow got on to the nature of our relationship—our "arrangement" as we euphemistically referred to it. Perhaps Leif was beginning to feel the artificiality of it; I was not, at that stage, sure. In fact, I was not quite certain what I was doing here in the first place: a forty-two-year-old Englishman on holiday in Rome with a twenty-five-year-old Norwegian. We made an odd couple, and I wondered if my obsession with the Roman fascination for his northern lights was not a way of distracting me from my own self-consciousness.

We had known each other only a few months, and had not yet spent as much time together as I would have liked. But when Leif had suggested the trip, as he'd not been to Rome before, I'd jumped at the opportunity to spend more time with him, to give ourselves the chance to get to know each other. I was only glad he hadn't suggested Venice. Leif in Venice . . .?

And there, in the unlikely setting of that suburban restaurant, he chose to bring up the very subject of our relationship.

"Are you happy with the way things work between us?"

"Yes—of course I am—we get on very well with each other, don't we?"

"Of course, but that's not what I meant. I'm talking about our agreement."

We were both somewhat wary of mentioning the terms under which we had started sleeping with each other; it made it all seem a little sordid, unromantic. Contrived.

"Well, it seems to work for me—does it not for you?"

"I'm not sure. In theory it does. It's the fracture between theory and practicalness that concerns me." It was rare for his English to be less than perfect; this fluency, coupled with an endearing smattering of colloquialisms, many originating from the States, usually made me feel that my own spoken English was clumsy. But tonight he seemed to be struggling to express himself.

I moved my legs under the table and squeezed his knee between mine for reassurance. "Tell me more! Tell me what you're feeling!"

One of the many things that excited me—intellectually—about Leif, was his ability to make me feel simultaneously in control and a complete child. Something about him, something about the age difference between us, coupled with his almost unnatural maturity in certain areas, brought into play my own contradictory feelings of adult and child, innocence and experience.

"It's not easy," he continued. "I thought I knew what I wanted from our relationship. I thought it was too soon for me to get emotionally involved with someone again. Before Tim I had experienced so little, and he taught me so much. In theory, I ought to want to have the opportunity to put some of that into action. To have some freedom now."

"But in practice?"

He looked at me as if about to tell me off for interrupting, but the waiter returned with our *antipasti*. I moved my knees and sat up.

"The rocket and parmigiano insalata?"

. . . . .

BACK IN THE club, Leif stands up suddenly. I assume he is about to look for the toilet, but he reaches for my hand and smiles, and I realize that the time has come for the next stage of the evening's entertainment. It's been many years since I've danced in a club. I still find it difficult not to refer to such places as discos, but I have, at least, learned that much. My understanding of the contemporary music scene became a little fuzzy somewhere after "New Romantic", and my work has allowed me little time for anything other than classical music. The last time I listened to pop standing up was at my fortieth birthday party, when I had done my best to surround myself with young things in a vain attempt to hang on to my thirties. Now a stab of nerves prods my overfull stomach as I realize that the rash promise to dance that I made earlier that evening, over our coffees, is being called in.

· · · · ·

OVER THOSE COFFEES, in the restaurant, it had become clear that the couple at the next table were having a row. A very restrained row, by Italian standards, but serious, nonetheless. I feared for the future of their relationship. She—stunningly beautiful—had stopped eating and waved her food away some time ago. He—coarser featured, and uncertain of himself—had continued with his food, perhaps through defiance, but the conversation had died out entirely. Eventually she had begun to fiddle with her mobile phone, and by the time his food was removed, he had lost any pretense of cool and had started quietly pleading with her. This seemed to be the last straw. She stood up, undramatically but decisively, and left, leaving him to deal with the bill and their life.

I wasn't sure how much of this my Leif was aware of. He was struggling with his own turmoil:

"My initial question was not about how we get on with each other."

"So what was it about?"

"Well . . . we had an agreement to start our relationship on open terms. I guess I need to know if you have taken advantage of that arrangement."

That word again. And the question I would rather not have answered. But at the same time I didn't want to lie to him. And in theory I had no need to.

"Well, yes, I have. Once. About a month ago. When we didn't see each other for those few weeks. It was totally meaningless."

Why did I feel it necessary to append this "confession" with so many excuses? Why did I confess in the first place—it would have been so much simpler to withhold the truth. I looked over the remains of my salad to try to gauge Leif's expression. He didn't meet my eyes.

"Why did you do it if it was meaningless?"

"Physical gratification? Self-esteem? I don't know! I thought *you* wanted our relationship to be open!"

. . . . .

THE CLUB IS populated by a comfortable mix of young, presumably gay, men; even younger, presumably straight, women; a few older, larger men—who in England or the States would have been termed "bears"; and a flamboyant, statuesque yet convincing, black transsexual. Leif leads me through this crowd until we reach the top of a staircase. I follow him down, surprised by the sudden drop in temperature as the stairs turn a sharp corner and change from concrete to stone. The coolness is refreshing after the heat of the sultry evening and of so many people crowded together in the ground-floor bar. I gaze around, trying to take in the sculptures standing on plinths, the ferns cleverly hanging in alcoves, all lit with tiny spotlights. I stumble on an uneven step, put my hand out to touch the rough wall to regain my balance, and I am instantly transported back to the catacombs that we'd visited earlier that day.

There it had also been a blessed relief to leave the midday heat of the entrance area and descend into the damp, cool, mustiness of the Catacombs of Santa Cecilia. We were herded into a long line of English speakers, and led down and down to the bottom of a long flight of stairs, where we were greeted by an elderly, white-haired man whose portable microphone-and-loudspeaker-combo (which looked like an antiquated hearing aid) and his badly-fitting false teeth combined to give the impression of a greater age and frailty than was the case. I had prepared myself for stilted English, spoken with a strong Italian accent, accompanied by a whistle (from false teeth or loudspeaker, or both). So it took me a few seconds to place his accent as American. And specifically New York. The surreality of all this was compounded by his irrepressible game show host jollity. I giggled, glanced at Leif. He was looking away, peering upward into the gloom, as if to calculate how far we had descended, how long it would take to re-emerge. I stifled my laughter and decided not to share the joke. It was in poor taste and would lose something in the translation. Instead, I turned my attention back to Father Simon, as his name badge told us he was called, who said, "And remember folks, we've never yet returned with the same number that we set out with!" His chilling chuckle echoed back up the staircase, as he led us on, and even further down, past rows of empty niches and labyrinthine cross passages.

The dance floor lies in a dungeon-like room at the foot of the club's stone staircase. Beyond it there seems to be another, darker room, but Leif leads me into the nearer chamber, nimbly dodging those already dancing, until he finds us a patch of stone floor on which we can establish ourselves and start this strange ritual. I am tense. I remember past attempts at losing myself in this kind of music, only to stumble, trip into a neighbor, and flee the dance floor in embarrassment. I listen to the beat. I watch as Leif swings easily, twists, and—effortlessly—launches himself into a response to the music. I copy him, trying to reproduce a scaled-down version, nothing too ambitious. My shoulders are too stiff. My feet are like lead. Surely everyone will stare at me. An old boy making a fool of himself with his young lover—probably rented, anyway. How come I'm the only one who feels self-conscious in this relationship—sorry—"arrangement"?

But then I begin to recognize the song, something I first danced to more than twenty years ago while still at university. And I begin to realize that no one *is* staring at me. And that my shoulders have dropped, and my arms feel freer, my legs lighter. And that Leif isn't laughing at me, isn't edging away in embarrassment, but is catching my eye easily, relaxed, happy, smiling. And I am dancing. Moving to the beat—twisting, curling, floating. And although I'm not quite sure of what I'm doing, or more to the point, why I'm doing it, I am enjoying myself, enjoying being with Leif in this strange place, enjoying sharing a room with a hundred other people, each of them also—apparently—happy, sharing something with all the others. And perhaps, at that moment, I begin to understand, for the first time ever, what the whole clubbing thing is all about.

I close my mind to any other, external worries, concentrate on the music, and look around me. Watching Leif occupying his space on the dance floor so confidently, so unselfconsciously, I am filled, once again, with a sense of amazement that we are here, together. The whole situation had crept up on me, somewhat by surprise. It felt less contrived than previous relationships, at which I'd surely tried too hard. This was unplanned, easier, and so lacking all that burden of expectation. I was simply here with someone who was beautiful, intelligent, sensitive, funny . . . and he was here simply because he chose to be with me.

And yet nothing, as ever, was entirely straightforward. Nothing was ever quite as it was meant to be. Here I am, dancing in a club in Rome on my birthday, falling in love. But I wasn't sure that I was allowed to, whether that was part of the deal.

. . . . .

THAT AFTERNOON, I had traipsed through the endless subterranean passageways of the catacombs feeling somewhat short-changed. The visit had been my own special request for the weekend. Although I'd been to Rome on several occasions over the years, I'd somehow never made it as far as the catacombs. This time it had seemed right. But now that I was actually here, in a queue of overheated Brits being led by a game show host, I felt cheated.

But then, at last, our group had spread out into a large, irregular, dimly-lit cave, at one end of which lay a strange statue of a twisted, contorted corpse. Santa Cecilia herself—patron saint of music—my muse, to whom I had come to pay homage. And somehow Father Simon had managed to suppress his showbiz jollity to relate the sorry tale of her conversion, her capture by the Romans, and her decapitation. She had died making two signs: one finger pointing on one hand, three on the other. One God and the Holy Trinity—Father, Son, and Holy Ghost. I was not religious—had stopped visiting church when a student—but the weight of the years and the strength of her faith moved me in that dim, dank sepulcher. As we filed into yet another tomb-lined corridor, I squeezed Leif's arm gently, glad of his silent company.

A few minutes later, as I emerged from a chamber containing a faded fresco depicting the Last Supper, I realized I couldn't find him among the group. I assumed he was nearby, probably lining up an artful shot full of light and shade with his fancy camera. Then, as I turned a particularly gloomy bend in the tunnel, I felt myself suddenly grabbed from behind, pulled backward. Thinking of Cecilia's fate and her Roman abductors, I stifled a cry, then realized it was Leif. He pulled me round, into another vault, and kissed me hard, passionately. Tense initially, worrying about the other visitors, about the sacrilege of it all, I looked around, startled. He held me, wouldn't let go, grinned. And I laughed, and suddenly understood. I returned the kiss.

· · · · ·

BACK TO TONIGHT, in the profane temple of *Testaccolo*, where more solid beings are the subject of adoration, I am beginning to tire. My legs, unaccustomed to this form of exercise, are aching. My shirt is drenched with sweat. I lean forward to shout in Leif's ear:

"I've had enough for a bit. I need a rest. You stay if you like. Come and find me when you're ready!"

He smiles, nods, winks, and then raises his arms to salute the music. I kiss him on the lips, and find a path through the heaving crowd of worshippers, back up to the bar, smiling smugly, absurdly happy. I extract a Peroni from the sullen bar boy, and make my way over to the second staircase in the club, this one leading upward. I climb up, out of the sultry, sticky heat, and once more find relief in cooler air, now on the roof of the building where an exotic terrace has been constructed, all jasmine and bamboo, overlooking Monte Testaccio itself in one direction, the hills of Trastevere in the other. The place is almost deserted. Why would anyone choose to roast in the crowds below when there is so much space and air up here? Perhaps I still wasn't entirely in tune with the clubbing mentality after all. I lean back against the cool, stuccoed wall. Close my eyes, swig my beer, breathe.

"It is nice up here, no?"

I jump, having thought myself alone. A few feet away, also leaning against the wall, also drinking from a bottle, stands a muscular man, handsome, dark. His shirt is tied around his waist, his smooth olive skin glistening in the dim light.

"It is private, no?"

Is this a come-on? I smile, amused.

"Very nice, yes. Very private. And cool after downstairs. It's too hot down there."

"But you were dancing well. You were happy down there. I saw you. With your *amico biondo*."

I laugh out loud now, surprising myself with its intensity. Chat show-host chuckles.

"Why you laugh? You laugh at me?"

The boy seems to flex his muscles, but not threateningly, more as a display of his masculinity, to assert himself. I raise my hands, defensively.

"No, no, I'm sorry. I'm not laughing at you. I'm sorry. I'm just happy. As you said. I'm very happy!"

"Then why you come up here all by yourself? You had a . . . a *disputa* . . . with your *amico*?"

"No, no. Leif is fine. I just needed some air."

"That is good. I think life is good also. It is good to be here with all the men and moving to the music and being happy together, no?"

I laugh again, nodding, unable even to begin to imagine how to correct his misunderstanding. Instead I ask his name.

"Vittorio. You can call me Vito. It is a good name, a strong name, no? That is why I do what I do. I am . . . Uh . . . how you say it . . . gladia*tor*?"

He, of course, emphasizes the last syllable, pronouncing the Italian word, which is, for once the same word as in English.

"Gladiator, yes. I mean, I think. How can you be? There are no gladiators these days. Except in films." I think of Russell Crowe. Not entirely dissimilar physically.

"Not film, no. I work as gladia*tor* in front of Colosseo. I stand in old . . . *costuma*? And then *americani*, *giapponese*, they take my photo. And pay me perhaps five euro, ten euro. Not the *inglese*, I think. You *inglesi*?"

"Yes. I'm English. I expect the English stand in the background and wait for you to pose for an American, and then take a crafty snap from a bad angle . . ."

"I no know. You not like *inglese*? You not proud of *Inghilterra*? Is a good country, I think. Thatcher? Madonna? David Beckham?"

I laugh yet again, allow my gaze to meet Vito's dark, eager eyes, to travel down to admire his sculpted, tanned chest. I'm sure he makes a very good living selling his body outside the Colosseum.

Suddenly I'm aware that a third person has climbed up to the terrace. Leif emerges from the shadows, and somewhat uncertainly comes over. I feel myself blushing.

"Hello you! Had a good dance? Here, meet Vito! He's a gladiator." I kiss Leif on the lips.

He looks at me questioningly. Vito wanders off, lazily, beer bottle dangling from his left hand, murmuring to himself, "*Molto biondo! Troppo biondo!*"

Leif pouts.

"Why is that the only characteristic of mine worth mentioning in this country?"

I put my arms round him, hug him tightly, say softly into his hair, "If only it were!"

We walk back to the hotel slowly, hand in hand, retracing our steps to the river, past the *trattoria*, closed up now and dark for the night. Further on, we pass a children's playground, deserted, except for the lone figure of a girl in a multicolored dress, carrying a parasol and gently tap dancing on the spot, on the concrete to one side of the swings. I cannot be sure she is really there.

. . . . .

LATER THAT NIGHT, early the next morning, as the sun began to rise over the Colosseum, where Vito is no doubt preparing to oil up and flex for another day, I curl up in bed beside Leif, totally satisfied, unbelievably happy, and yet thoroughly calm. I mold myself to his form, marveling at how my knees fit into the back of his legs, how my arm drapes over his body at the narrowing of his waist, how my hand finds his in the shelter of his neck. Two fragments found lying on the ground. Picked up, placed together, made one by the strange events of an extraordinary day. Potsherds. Embracing Leif.

TURBULENT
TIMES

TEA FOR TWO

JIM VAN BUSKIRK

"**WHAT DO YOU** want to do today?" I asked Allen while we were still lying in bed.

"We could install the wire for your stereo speaker."

I considered his offer. This was a task we'd been putting off since I moved into my new apartment a few weeks ago. "Or we could take a drive to someplace merry," he suggested.

It took a minute before I remembered that Allen could talk while he was still asleep.

"Let's not waste this beautiful day working on my speakers," I said, getting up to survey the panoramic view through the bedroom windows. It was a sunny San Francisco spring day. "Let's go somewhere 'merry'."

"Where do you want to go?" Allen sat up a little.

"Let me call the Ritz-Carlton at Half Moon Bay to see if anyone has canceled," I said, walking toward the phone. I had tried to make a reservation for afternoon tea there days earlier but had been told the room was fully committed and that we would be placed on a waiting list. "I hope this works," I said as punched in the ten-digit number. "We could drive down the coast slowly and then have tea." I looked over at Allen while I waited for the hostess to check her book, until she was able to tell me, yes, they had a four o'clock seating.

I had wanted to do this for months, ever since my friend Claudia and I had driven down the coast to Santa Cruz and stopped at the new hotel. We had marveled at its large scale, so at odds with the spectacular setting on the dramatic bluff overlooking the ocean.

When we wandered around the warm interior spaces with their dramatic views, I was inspired. "I'll bring Allen here for afternoon tea on Valentine's Day," I told Claudia.

"What a good idea," she concurred, impressed with my romantic idea. She seemed a bit rueful that her own husband wouldn't have thought of it.

But when I called for a reservation, inexplicably the hotel wasn't taking reservations for Valentine's Day. The alternate date I chose turned out to be the weekend I was moving into my new apartment, so it wasn't until now, late March, that Allen and I drove down the coast in anticipation of a lovely afternoon.

As the freeway twisted toward the coast, I noticed wisps of white clouds licking the tips of the hills. "Uh, oh," I groaned. "Looks like the coast may be socked in." And sure enough, heading south down Highway One, the left side of the road was sunny and clear, and the right side was foggy and gray. The dramatic demarcation across the expanse of asphalt seemed surreal as we continued south.

Each time we rounded a bend in the road I kept hoping that the sun would be strong enough to burn through the fog.

"We'll enjoy it whatever the weather's like," said Allen politely, and we fell silent.

As I the drove I looked over at Allen, appreciating his curly blond hair and sweet countenance. I thought back to how we had met. He was stage-managing a concert produced by Lawrence, my ex-boyfriend and now best friend; I was helping "front of house." I thought I'd noticed a bit of a buzz between us that night, but gave it little thought. A few weeks later, I received an e-mail from Allen congratulating me on my essay about Gustave Caillebotte on the Web. Allen had apparently stumbled upon my article on the French impressionist painter while playing with his new computer. He invited me to lunch, and I accepted. The lunch was pleasant, but uneventful. We talked of singers and shows and gay gossip, but not much of substance, and not much about ourselves. Then he started extending offers of free theater tickets.

"I think Allen likes you," Lawrence counseled me one day.

"I thought so too," I admitted. "But . . ." Frequently, when I dropped Allen off in front of his apartment building after an evening out, he'd leap from the car almost, it seemed, before I got to his corner. There was no invitation to come up, and not even any awkward, lingering "good night." I didn't give it much thought. I was dating someone else, but I continued to accept his platonic overtures.

After about a year of this, and once my other relationship had ended, Allen invited me over to demonstrate the wondrous capabilities of his new DVD player. "Come for dinner. We'll have a DVD party," he promised.

"A BVD party?" I asked, escalating the situation with faux misunderstanding.

"If you'd like," he said suggestively.

When he discovered I'd never seen *The Red Shoes*, Allen loaded his favorite film into the machine. Sitting together on the small sofa watching the movie, I started playing footsy. At first I couldn't tell if he was responding. Was I misreading this situation? Slowly, almost imperceptibly at first and then more noticeably we rubbed our feet against each other. One thing led to another and soon we were on his bed wearing only our boxer shorts. Suddenly the horseplay stopped.

"I have something to tell you," Allen said seriously.

"Okay," I said. A knot stuck in my stomach. "Let's have it."

"I have a partner."

Lawrence had told me that Allen had a long-term partner. But there seemed to be no sign of him and Allen had never mentioned him. Now I learned that Allen and Tom had been together for twenty years. Tom currently lived in Portland and they saw each other a few times a year for several days or weeks at a time.

Summoning a nonchalance I wasn't sure I felt, I said, "That's okay with me. If it's okay with you." It seemed to be, so we continued. I figured Allen just wanted to have his way with me. That was fine by me. He could count me as a conquest as long as I got laid.

We both got what we apparently wanted and I was impressed when he gallantly got dressed and walked me to my car.

A few days later, Allen arrived at work unannounced bearing a card and flowers. How sweet, I thought. Then he called to set up lunch. More cards, flowers, gifts, dates. Maybe I was wrong, I thought. Maybe this wasn't just a one-night stand.

So the affair continued, with theater and concerts and lunches and watching DVDs, usually followed by sex. Our relationship seemed to be mostly based on the sex, since our conversations weren't particularly intellectually stimulating. This was surprising since Allen was a playwright and a director. He didn't read much, except newspapers and magazines.

"I *can* read," he said with mock haughtiness when I teased him. "I just choose not to." But he was wise in other ways.

How did I feel about having an affair with a "married" man? It certainly wasn't the first time. This was only the most recent demonstration of the unavailability to which I seem attracted in men.

"I'm not leaving Tom," Allen reminded me repeatedly. Was that to reassure me? It worked. It made it safe enough for me to know that there would be no talk of monogamy or marriage or moving in together. Topics that had terrified me with former boyfriends. It took a long time to realize he wasn't going anywhere. But I was; I was growing closer to him and to myself.

Allen continually told me how handsome I was. "I can't believe you don't have a boyfriend. I'll be your training wheels. I'll be your boyfriend until you find one of your very own." I wasn't quite sure exactly what that meant, but the flowers and gifts kept coming, the cards signed "Fondly, Allen." He called me many mornings, and often during the day, and always in the evening. We got together frequently for a quick tumble in bed, even if we didn't end up spending the night together. "I'm fond of you," he told me often.

Then Allen started referring to me as his boyfriend. At first it made me uncomfortable. I had been content to be the "Back Street" boyfriend, hidden in the shadows, like Susan Hayward in the movie of that name. But Allen had held my hand and kissed me in public, presented me to friends, referred to me as his boyfriend. "But you already have a boyfriend," I protested, bewildered.

"Do you think a person can only have one boyfriend?" Harvey, my therapist asked.

I thought for a while. "I guess I do." I was surprised. Where did these beliefs come from? Allen may not have set off fireworks when we were together, not like the feverish frenzy I usually felt when I met someone new to whom I was attracted. This had started so slowly that I hadn't even noticed that it seemed to be turning into something significant.

"I can't see it coming," I said, describing the ongoing deepening of our relationship. "I don't even see it while it's happening. It's as if I can only see it in the rear view mirror, once it's passed. Then it's safe to see it, to say it."

What Allen had to offer came in subtle, unexpected ways. There was the time he refused to let me dismiss his offer to accompany me when I went for an MRI. "I'm coming with you," he insisted. Thank goodness he did because I freaked out, my claustrophobia triggered by the coffin-like canister. It required several aborted attempts at sliding me into the tube before we found that only if he hung on to my toes could I endure the almost the five-minute episodes before being pulled out. I hadn't wanted to accept his generosity. I thought I could do it alone; didn't realize I needed him to help me get through. The lessons slowly sank in and the relationship continued.

It was tough when Tom was in town. Even though he had told Tom what was going on, I was not to call Allen at home, his calls were surreptitious and infrequent, our dates reduced to lunchtime trysts at the nearby ostensibly-straight hot tubs. I had trouble adjusting after having enjoyed such a level of intimacy. Over the months that we had spent time together, I had become angry and pulled away, become hurt and pulled away, felt abandoned and pulled away, but always Allen was there. He didn't get defensive, he didn't argue, he didn't explain or remind me that I knew what I was getting into. He listened, he acknowledged, he agreed, and together we developed a plan to avoid the particular situation that had triggered my anxiety. Sometimes the strategy worked, other times it needed tweaking, but slowly I learned I didn't have to hide myself from him. That he was reliable, trustworthy, and dependable.

I spoke to Harvey about not understanding what was happening between us, and surprisingly he encouraged me to pursue it. "But what about Tom?" I asked every week.

"This isn't about Tom," Harvey inevitably replied. "This is about you."

"But . . ." I'd sputter, trying to accept my inability to understand. I didn't want to jeopardize their relationship, but I did like spending time with Allen.

Neither of us had ever uttered the L word, until one afternoon during one of Tom's extended visits and we were having "lunch." Lying naked in the seamy setting of the wood-paneled room of the Central Hot Tubs, amid the threadbare sheet, cardboard towels, and smell of chlorine, I held him in my arms and looked into his eyes.

"I love you," I said, trembling.

"You mean you're fond of me," he responded. And then he looked at me intently. "I love you too." We looked into each other's eyes and held on tightly.

We had crossed a line, now there was no going back. I continued to get upset whenever Tom came to town and I felt the connection with Allen dissipate.

"He has integrity," Harvey said, after I recounted yet another of my many meltdowns. An odd word under the circumstances, but it felt right.

The powerful and painful opening and closing of my heart continued. At one point, in the candlelit corner of dark downtown cocktail lounge, I sobbed. "I didn't mean to fall in love with you," I wailed.

Allen just held my hand and let me cry.

"I can't do this," I continued. He held my hand tighter.

"If you want to break up with me," he said softly, "let's do it together. Don't run away and do it on your own. We'll do it together."

I stopped crying for a minute, and looked at him in disbelief. Was this for real? This sensitivity and strength. This apparently unconditional love that I had heard about but never believed in, and certainly never experienced. Allen smiled at me, the candlelight catching his eyes, causing them to sparkle. He was so sweet and handsome. With my puffy, red eyes and runny nose I felt unattractive, and ridiculous. I blew my nose, again. I realized that no matter what happened, everything was going to be just fine.

· · · · ·

NOW I WATCHED the road as the fog and the sun continued to dance capriciously against each other, neither giving way for more than a few feet. Wisps of ethereal whiteness wafted and waned in a celestial tango as we chatted about the scenery, or lack of it.

We turned off the highway and headed west through the green undulating golf course. The fog was getting thicker. Damn, I thought, we won't be able to see a thing. The hotel loomed dimly before us, an ungainly edifice on the steep headlands. From a distance it looked like an immense condominium complex or the huge movie set of an east coast hotel. Its scale was so inappropriate for the spectacular natural setting, it was little wonder its construction had been controversial. I drove past the valet parking sign and through the curving streets reminiscent of a suburban housing development, looking for a place to park. NO PARKING signs were posted everywhere.

I suddenly remembered that the reservations person had told me that valet parking was validated. I turned around and drove up the grand circular drive to the hotel portico.

"A bit pretentious," I muttered to Allen. He didn't say a word.

The liveried valet opened the car door and handed me a stub. "Checking in?" he asked.

"No, just having afternoon tea," I replied, getting out of the car.

"Your tea will cover all but three dollars of the parking."

"I was told the parking was validated."

"It is, except for the three dollars."

I could feel my face get hot. I took a breath. "That's not what the reservation person said."

The attendant quickly acquiesced, but I couldn't resist making one final comment. "You might want to inform the people who answer the telephone not to be giving out misinformation."

"What was all that?" Allen asked, getting out of the car. More attendants opened the double-leaded glass doors for us as we walked into the luxurious hotel.

"Oh, nothing." I'd hoped he hadn't heard my exchange. I hurried him inside. We walked down the polished marble floors of the handsomely appointed hallway looking for the library where tea was to be served.

There was no maitre d' with whom to check in, so we stood in the wood-paneled room waiting to be acknowledged. We saw several servers in a variety of uniforms, their hierarchical codes eluding us. They passed us without a word or nod. Through the picture windows we saw a wall of swirling fog.

"That's where the incredible view would be," I pointed out. Eventually we flagged an employee and were seated in a cozy room overlooking a larger space, beyond which was the nonexistent view.

We sat surveying the intimate surroundings. The cream-colored damask tablecloth, white porcelain dishes with subtle floral motif, and the classical design of the silverware were all high quality. A small glass vase held a single pink rose, the brightest color in the otherwise muted surroundings. There were only four other tables in the alcove, filled with family or friends, overwhelmingly heterosexual. Finally our tea sandwiches, scones, and *petits fours* were brought to us on a three-tiered tray.

"Here is your high tea," the server said sweetly. She graciously poured Allen's orange spice tea. "It reminds me of my grandmother," he said. Then my blue sapphire tea, "available exclusively at Ritz-Carlton" according to the menu, was poured. I half expected it to be blue in color.

"It's not high tea," I hissed, as soon as she'd left. "High tea is a working class mid-afternoon meal. This is afternoon tea. Everyone makes that mistake. You'd think for twenty-six dollars a pop they could get it right." I rolled my eyes.

Allen smiled. He lifted his teacup. "Here's to Valentine's Day." I raised mine to meet his. I looked directly into his eyes. "And you are one of my Valentines."

I returned my cup to its saucer, and glared at him. "Why did you have to say that?" I had planned this outing as a romantic interlude.

"I don't know." He lowered his head, murmured softly.

"Being with you has been incredibly healing," I began. "And then you catch me off guard by saying something very wounding."

Allen remained silent.

"I wasn't even going to bring up Valentine's Day," I continued. I tried to prevent the tears I felt welling. I didn't want this special afternoon to be ruined. And I certainly didn't want to think about Tom. "I was going to say that it's been almost a year that we've been seeing each other, and I've had a most marvelous time."

"I have, too," Allen agreed.

"I know you have *two*," I said with mock frustration. "Why do you insist on bringing it up?"

Allen laughed. I laughed too at having successfully diffused the situation. Our eyes sparkled.

He leaned over to give me a kiss. "I'm sorry."

I brushed at the wetness around my eyes, and smiled. "So how do you like this Devonshire cream?" I looked around the room to see if anyone had witnessed our emotional display.

"It's like a mix of whipped cream and butter," he said, slathering more of what looked like mayonnaise from the tiny ramekin onto his miniature scone. Then he happily spread a little of the lemon curd on top of that.

We quickly resumed our tender mood, laughing about the ill-clad people wandering through the hotel. We discussed our favorites from among the many small delicacies we'd been served. I knew Allen didn't care for cucumbers so without a word I exchanged my smoked salmon sandwich for his cucumber one. We agreed that the scones were light and flaky. I asked for more hot water for my teapot, and then went to the bathroom. I surveyed the other people, trying not to feel somehow superior. When I returned, I realized again how handsome and sweet Allen was. How his resolute steadfastness was exactly what was called for. We agreed that whiling away the afternoon sipping tea and nibbling tiny comestibles was the height of hedonism. Without either of us saying anything, it was apparent that something significant had subtly shifted.

We lingered a while longer after we had finished off the last of the tiered tray of goodies, savoring the deliciousness of the moment as we sipped the now tepid tea. Then we acknowledged that we were ready, and rose to wander through the overly ornate hotel. Exiting the hotel's large glass doors, we took a stroll along the paved path edging the promontory. We could hear but scarcely see the surf pounding below. We laughed ruefully at the opalescent fog that surrounded us. After being buffeted by the damp mist for twenty minutes, we went back into the hotel.

Standing in a secluded alcove adjacent to a floor-to-ceiling window, I put my arms around Allen. He turned toward me and kissed me. "Thank you for the tea. It was lovely."

"It nearly wasn't," I said.

"Yes, thanks for so cleverly saving the day."

"Well, I decided I didn't want to go into high drama." I kissed him.

"It wouldn't have been high drama," Allen corrected. "High drama is a working class phenomenon. It would have been afternoon drama."

I kissed him again. We held hands as we walked back through the hotel hallways to retrieve the car, ready for our drive home.

THE MAN I LOVE, THE MAN I LEFT

ANTHONY PAULL

THE PLANE IS landing in five minutes. His plane. Him: the man I love, the man I left. We have a date. We're going to a fancy restaurant that serves flowers instead of salad. But I'm not at the airport to pick him up. I'm waiting for him to come to me. In a shoddy apartment over two thousand miles from the place I call home, I'm waiting, I'm wondering, and right now I'm completely lost.

No one told me L.A. apartments come without refrigerators. I learned this the day of my arrival, the same day my best friend Erin and I relocated from Florida to a cesspool just north of Hollywood. Erin wanted to work in film. And me, I just wanted to work.

Typical L.A. twenty-nothings, we had no money. And I had this brilliant idea: Let's kill two birds with one stone. Let's cure our weight and money problems simultaneously. Let's live without purchasing a fridge.

"Agreed," Erin said, finding the thought inspiring. And soon we were eating and drinking out of cans. Cans we found at the dollar store. Cans of warm diet soda. Cans of slippery noodles that slide through your body faster than the lo mein at a cheap Chinese buffet.

At first, the plan worked well. Sure, we lived in a smog-filled wasteland. Sure, our careers were going nowhere. But we didn't care. We were on our own and we were free. The weight was flying off, and soon we had celebrity bodies, bodies that any Hollywood star would wire shut his or her jaw to emulate. Bodies that made life worth living.

The man I love—the man I left—he's going to knock on my door in less than an hour. This morning he flew two thousand miles to see me. This afternoon, he suffered two hours of L.A. traffic. "Not a problem," he says. He'll do it anytime for me. Beautiful me, beautiful unemployed me who works out at the gym instead of working a full-time job, who recently graduated from Who Gives a Shit College and has not a clue what to do.

I'm not sure what he loves about me. Lately, it's hard to feel lovable. Especially since I haven't made one new friend in six months of L.A. living. Especially since I haven't been out of the apartment for a week.

Luckily, he phoned bright and early each and every morning. Like the rising sun, this is how I soon learned it was a brand new day.

How are you doing? Have you made any friends? Have you found any work?

"Of course I found work," I told him. "Haven't you heard? I'm the newest coolest extra on the scene. Didn't you see me? Didn't you notice the fag in the background of *Mighty Morphin' Power Rangers* this week?"

Yes, that was me—the fag who never earned a speaking line . . . The fag who blended in with the bookcase in the library scene . . . The fag who should have known to wear a bolder color . . .

Fast forward to now—today. I'm still not speaking. This second, this very second, I'm in much too much pain to speak. Not emotional pain, but physical pain. It's embarrassing really. Most people would know better than to speak of such pain. But me, I'm not one of those people. The problem is: who in L.A. would care enough to listen?

The man I love—the man I left—he'd listen. But I can't tell him. No. It's not proper. Soon, he'll arrive for our date. And I'll be the skeleton who won't let the skeleton out of the closet. I'll be the famished fag standing in an apartment with no furniture, no refrigerator, wondering why a purple, painful bump has magically appeared on his butt.

"Damn. Is this one of those STDs?" I finally ask Erin. Sucking down a Styrofoam cup of instant noodles, she takes the empathetic vibe and asks me about the last time I fed the toilet. Did it hurt? Did I strain? Do I have enough fiber in my diet? "Not unless they started putting it in SpaghettiOs," I reply.

Knock. Knock. Knock. The man I love is at the door. And Erin being Erin—she tells me to drop my pants and bend over so she can take a look. "To help verify my diagnosis," she tells me.

"No, you can't look!" I scream. "Are you nuts?"

"Relax. It's probably a hemorrhoid."

Hemorrhoid? Lovely. So much for my power bottom routine, I tell myself. But before I freak, the man I love opens the door, and I smile. "Hey shining star," he says, kissing me. His cologne smells like the ocean, and when he hugs me I'm reminded of home, the feeling of being connected.

Momentarily losing focus of my pain, I instead focus on him. The brown of his eyes, the way his lips form a heart. I ask myself, why did I leave him? Why am I here? And why am I skeletal?

Later in the rental car, he calms me. "Who knows? Maybe that look will get you more parts," he says, driving us to the fancy restaurant that serves flowers instead of salad. "But from what I'm seeing, it looks like you could put on a few pounds. Are you feeling okay?" The man I left—he's using that caring voice. The voice that tells me he loves me. Six months ago, the voice that made me run.

Right now, my mind is doing the running. Running down a list of excuses as to why I need to stop at the pharmacy. The purchase of hemorrhoid ointment isn't one of those excuses.

Holding his hand, I'm half-sitting on the passenger seat as one would sit on a public toilet, and I'm telling half-truths. That I'm bored with dining out, that maybe we should skip it, and that maybe we should stop at the corner store and buy a pack of smokes before we make any more headway.

He's suspicious, and a tad confused. But then again, maybe this is why he loves me. He never can figure me out. Just when he thinks I'm sane, I distract him by acting loopy. Right now, I have him running through hoops.

This very moment he's behind me, and I'm dodging him down aisle three of Such and Such Pharmacy. He thinks I'm being cute. That I'm playing hide-and-seek. But really, I'm just plain hiding. Hiding while I seek hemorrhoid ointment—hiding the most recently painful of my many flaws.

My new life is supposed to have made me independent. But in aisle three of Such and Such Pharmacy, I'd clutch a stranger for a moment of not feeling so alone. This is me. I feel ugly and isolated. I know that he is my home. That he is running down the next aisle, trying to find me, trying to love me, but I refuse to show him I care. Six months ago, I can't say why I left, but I know the decision was right.

When the man I love finds me, I'm hiding the ointment in my hand, and he playfully grabs my butt. The pain is vicious, but I continue smiling. I can't help it. He makes me smile through the pain. He makes the pain feel safe. Like the pain is part of being human. Like the pain is part of being in love. "Go on. Meet me in the car," I tell him.

He gives me a curious look. "Why? What's up?"

Tenderly kissing his cheek, I whisper something about every good boy needing a good secret. That being a good boy, I need a few minutes alone. That in time, he'd be in for a really nice surprise.

That's me, full of surprises.

Surprise—I love you.

Surprise—I have a purple bump on my ass.

They're both the same. They're equally haunting. They're equally ruinous. But I'm not ruined yet. I have my ointment. I have my man waiting in a rental car. And I cover my tracks by purchasing a pack of smokes.

"Smoking again?" he asks, as I enter the car.

I look away, telling him I detest cigarettes—telling him that cigarettes are a way for lonely people to inhale death a little sooner. Telling him I never want to be *that* lonely. Then I think maybe I am *that* lonely. Why else would I be purchasing cigarettes? "Don't worry," he assures me. "You're never truly alone. Not if you have me in your life." We're driving down a busy L.A. street, and for some reason, I believe him. Maybe it's his firm tone. Maybe it's the fact I hear forever in his voice.

In a moment of clarity, I admit it to myself: this is why I left him—I'm afraid of forever. I'm afraid of having him, holding him, and losing him all at once. I'm afraid of being vulnerable. I'm afraid of growing up. I'm afraid of losing control.

Here we are driving toward the restaurant, but all I can think about is home. "Turn the car around," I tell him.

"What? You don't want to eat?"

"No, I want to go back to the apartment."

He doesn't ask why. He knows I'm upset. So he makes a U-turn. And I think, maybe I *do* have some control. Maybe he'll let me take the wheel sometimes. Maybe this is why I love him.

He's patient with me. He listens. He allows me to be angry. He knows that relationships are not a fairy tale even if you're a fairy, and that sometimes a good love story has a twisted ending.

We're still writing our story, he and I. And this chapter begins with the concluding portion of our date. We're back at the apartment, and the apartment is empty—no furniture, no fridge, no roommate. But to me, it no longer *feels* empty. Neither does my stomach. Not with the man I love ordering pizza in the next room. His voice makes the apartment full, as if there was a huge love seat in the center of the living room, covering the cigarette stains on the carpet, covering the ex-lover stains on my heart.

I've been hurt in the past, it's true. But I can't allow this hurt to hurt me anymore. I'm in enough pain right now. I'm in the bathroom making minor adjustments—soothing the savage purple beast, if you will. And through the door, I hear him—the man I love. He's reciting a list of fruits and vegetables over the phone. "Green peppers, broccoli, tomatoes, mushrooms, pineapple—load the pizza with every color of the rainbow," he says.

And suddenly, I know *he* knows. He knows I'm not healthy. He knows I need fiber, and he knows I have a hemorrhoid. Ultimately, he's knows he's not going to score tonight.

The interesting part is he's not leaving; he's not running like I ran six months ago. He's not telling me he needs more time. That he has to find himself. In fact, he's not saying a word.

This is love. When I'm at my worst, he returns me to my best. And when I feel alone, he assures me I'll never be *truly* alone as long as I choose to have him there.

Here, there, right now I want him everywhere . . .

"Everything okay?" he asks, gently knocking on the bathroom door.

Me, I'm knocking myself on the head. Realizing I'm stupid, realizing I'm crying, and realizing it's not from the pain, but from the joy of having him there. "Be out in a minute," I tell him. But truthfully, the minute lasts an hour. One hour of sitting alone but not feeling alone. One hour of realizing I no longer have to run. One hour later, the pizza finally arrives.

"Oh, I forgot to tell you," I laugh, losing the lights and lighting a candle. Struggling to be the man, he's on the living room carpet, manhandling the gooey pizza without making a mess. "Remember the surprise I promised you earlier?" Pushing the pizza aside, he makes space for me. He welcomes me. His lap becomes my cushion and I sit down. "I've decided to move back home."

FAREWELLS

LAST DATE

RICK R. REED

I'M DRIVING NORTH on Florida State Route 75. It's August and the flat land stretching out on either side of the highway looks baked. The slash pines, palms, and cypress trees stand like stalwart sentinels against the blistering sun: brave.

The car hums along, the whirr of the air conditioning compressor keeping me company. I'm too jazzed to listen to music.

I'm on my way to a date with Jim. It's been a while since I've seen him, since he moved from the Tampa Bay area up north to Raiford, a good three hours away. I can't blame Jim for the move (it wasn't his choice), but it's been hard not being able to see him for the past month. Oh sure, we've written and Jim's a great one for letters, especially since he can draw hilarious caricatures of the people he's meeting in his new home.

But there's a disturbing edge to his letters, too, and I know some of these people have been less than kind to Jim. The name-calling, for one thing, breaks my heart. But thank God Jim has a sense of humor, otherwise I don't know how he'd get through each day.

I know he's been hanging on for this date, which we've had planned for a while.

Finally, an afternoon with Jim. I didn't know, four months ago, that I would grow to love him so quickly.

I drive on, the broad expanses of rough grass and hearty trees replaced every so often by strip malls and towns with names like Ocala. The pavement shimmers before me in the heat. My tires hum. An armadillo hurries alongside the road. A mosquito splats against the windshield, leaving a tiny swath of blood.

I remember the first time I met Jim. It was another blistering summer day (funny how in my memories of the two years I lived in Florida, it's always summer, even when the memory took place in December or February). Jim and I had been set up and these kinds of dates always put me on edge: they never worked out.

When Jim answered the door, I was sure that this set-up date would be like all the others: completely inappropriate. Other people never seemed to have the capacity to pick someone that I would choose on my own.

And this guy who opened the door immediately put me on my guard. I mean, I enjoy a good drag show at the local bar as much as the next guy, but here in Brandon, Florida—a suburb of Tampa full of kids, trimmed lawns, and swimming pools—a smart little black dress and pearls just seemed out of place, especially on a very handsome blond man with great blue eyes and a nice, tight build.

But there was Jim, all smiles and beckoning me to come inside. I went into the little bungalow where he lived with a roommate, who was at work. The place was typical Florida: one-story, stucco, with a schefflera bush in the front yard, and that peculiar, tougher-than-nails, fire ant-infested grass on the front lawn. Inside, pastel walls and beige furniture completed the picture. *The Golden Girls* could have used the place for a set.

And there was Jim, smiling at me in his sensible matron's outfit and just putting the finish creases on a little ironing he was doing just before I rang the bell. The whole scene made me think of a cross between June Cleaver and RuPaul.

I wasn't sure what to say. But that really didn't matter, because Jim was more than ready to take over (once he'd made certain I had a fruity cocktail in my hand, even though it wasn't yet noon), telling me all about his recent move down here from Chicago (I had the same story to tell, but I wasn't to learn until much later how very different our respective moves to the sunshine state were), his love for Barbra (need I add a last name here?), and how his health was improving under the abundant Florida sun.

I learned fast that day that clothes don't always make the man and that Jim would turn out to be one of the bravest men I'd ever met.

. . . . .

IT'S BEEN A long drive and I'm glad to finally be pulling up in front of Jim's new home. Raiford is in north central Florida; typical of the state, but not the kind of look one usually associates with Florida (white sand beaches, aqua-marine waters, palm trees swaying in the salty breeze). Raiford is kind of grim and parched looking, especially the wide open spaces where Jim's new home sits. It's surrounded by dry brown grass, stretching infinitely to a blazing blue sky, where the sun beats down, relentless.

Jim's new home is surrounded by a tall fence, with no nod to adornment. (Jim, with his graphic design background and his love for the visual arts did not, I'm sure, approve). This fence was made of foreboding chain link and twice the height of a good-sized man, topped with razor-sharp circles of barbed wire. The only thing that looks halfway decent is the curving arch over the entrance drive and the stone monument just beside it. The arch tells visitors, in curving steel, that this is the Florida State Prison. The stone monument spells it out further: Department of Corrections, Florida State Prison.

This is where they send the big boys: the felons.

I can't imagine Jim inside. He's been hanging on for our date. I can't wait to see him.

. . . . .

WHEN JIM AND I went on our first date (after our getting-acquainted morning cocktail hour at his house) we went to Fort DeSoto beach, a beautiful stretch of white sand just off of St. Petersburg Beach. Because it's in a state park, the beach is backed up not by high-rises with balconies overlooking the Gulf of Mexico, but with a view that nature intended. Instead of bricks and mortar and the attendant Florida tourists, Fort DeSoto beach has only sand dunes, sea grass, and mangroves as a backdrop. It's another blazing hot day. I've brought lunch for Jim and me (and a thermos of mai tais, Jim's favorite) and we spend the entire afternoon listening to the waves roll in and watching a matronly pair wade along the shoreline, net bags in hand, collecting starfish and shells.

Jim tells me about the last job he had before he went on this extended period of unemployment, when he worked as a graphic designer. He tells me about what led to his dismissal: picking up a stranger one night and bringing him back to his workplace. Out of lube, and always imaginative, Jim went into his supervisor's cube and found some very creative use for the waxy and slippery substance those in the cosmetology trade call lipstick. The couple made quite a mess, not the least of which was Jim's being fired the next day.

Jim was like that: a little imp, unable to play by the rules.

Life has a way of biting those who go against its conventions by biting them in the ass.

· · · · ·

GETTING INTO THE Florida State Prison is a lot easier than getting out, but there are some obstacles. In order to arrange for my date with Jim, I had to go through the chaplain, who put me on the very short list of visitors who could come and visit him. Not that there was a long list of admirers waiting to be put on that list; so far only Jim's family had come to check him out in his new digs—and they had made the trip all the way from Downer's Grove, Illinois. Once inside the prison, I had to go through an anteroom, where I had to sign in and then subject myself to being frisked, right down to removing my boots to ensure I wasn't securing a file in the heel or something. I understood the precautions, silly as they were. Yet Jim was in no shape to escape, even if I had somehow managed to smuggle in everything he would need to slip through Raiford's well-guarded walls.

Security hadn't been as tight for my last couple of dates with Jim, which had taken place at the Hillsborough County Jail. There, things weren't as grim, or as lonely. I would line up with a whole room full of chattering visitors, get checked in, and then be off to converse with Jim through a wall of Plexiglas, under the admiring eyes of some of the other inmates. Jealousy is such a petty thing, and particularly annoying when you're trying to have an intimate moment with your date, while those behind him wonder what it would take to make you their bitch.

But that was before Jim's case was adjudicated and they sent him north, to the state prison. That was before Jim began to get really sick.

I'm led by a guard down a colorless hallway to the prison infirmary. I know this will be my last date with Jim and it's hard not to recall all the laughs we shared before he was caught (he had violated his parole in Illinois, where he had been convicted of grand theft auto): at various beaches along the Gulf of Mexico, in Cuban restaurants, just listening to music at my apartment.

It's also hard not to remember the additional details that brought him here: how, in a fit of depression, he had set fire to his roommate's house. What did he have to be depressed about, anyway? He was only dying from AIDS (this was in the early 1990's and the drug cocktails that would keep many living full lives were still beyond the horizon), isolated, and on the run from the law. Why be sad when he could number his friends (me) on one finger? Why be sad when my friendship was not borne out of our common love for the arts and sarcastic observations about life, but instead courtesy of the Tampa AIDS Network, where I had volunteered to be an AIDS buddy and was assigned to Jim?

I wasn't sure I wanted to see Jim. He had written me, before he was confined to the infirmary, about how the other inmates taunted him and called him Spot, because of the Kaposi's sarcoma lesions that covered him from head to toe and continued, even now, to eat his fragile body and soul alive. I didn't know what to expect. The last time I had seen him, he was still vibrant, still Jim: a little blond man with a quick smile and bottomless kindness.

I knew he had deteriorated . . . and I knew it was going to be bad.

Jim was alone in the room of the infirmary where they had done, I suppose, what they could to ensure his comfort. Other beds awaited other inmates, with maladies less deadly, I hoped, than Jim's.

And there he was. Asleep. He looked frail and vulnerable, not at all what you'd imagine if you thought of the terms convicted felon or state pen inmate. His face, once tanned and vibrant, was covered with purple sores. My Jim had turned into a monster in the short time that had elapsed since we last saw each other.

He turned to me and opened his eyes. At least his eyes, blue as those waters we had once sat beside, had stayed the same. It took him a minute or two to recognize me, but when he did, he smiled. I moved close to the bed and took his hand. With my other hand, I touched his forehead, where a fever raced around inside, hot as the air outside these prison walls.

I don't remember what we talked about on our last date. Probably not much; Jim drifted in and out of sleep while I stood beside him, sometimes even in the middle of a sentence: mine or even his own. He did manage to tell me about his parents' visit the day before, how his mother had collapsed in grief the moment she saw him.

I wanted this last time of ours together to be meaningful. But what, really, is there to say, at life's end? I leaned in close and kissed him, my cheek brushing up against one of the lesions. It felt crusty.

The only thing left to say, really, at the end of life, or even the end of a perfect date, are three words: "I love you." Jim whispered back, "I love you, too," and then he fell asleep.

I crept away.

Jim died the next day. The chaplain very kindly told me, when

he called, that he thought Jim had hung on long enough to see
me. I hung up the phone and slipped outside to my patio, and
looked across the surface of the pond just steps away. A wind rip-
pled across the deep green water, making the grass at the water's
edge sway. A white ibis pecked at something along the shore.

I thought of a silly drawing Jim had sent me a couple months
ago. It was a colored pencil caricature of a fat middle-aged woman
I had written about; she was naked and riding a surfboard. Jim had
called it "Amelia's Hawaiian Adventure."

The picture made me laugh when all I really wanted to do was
cry. But my eyes were dry. Maybe it was just Jim's influence, as he
looked down, trying to replace grief with hilarity. I laughed until
I was almost breathless and had to sit down, cross-legged, on the
concrete.

Finally my laughs turned to sobs and I faced away from the
pond and toward the sliding glass doors. The glass was bright
with sun and I swore I could see Jim reflected there. He mouthed
some words and I strained to read them through my tears. "Glad
you could drop by." I swallowed, containing myself, and thought:
*me too, Jim. Someone else might think our last date was kind of sucky,
but for me it was perfect. After all, a perfect date is marked by a timeless
connection and an intimacy borne of true love. Maybe I didn't get the
chance to bring you flowers or candy, but this date we had . . . well, it will
be the one that will always stand out in my mind as my best, because I
like to think that I sent you off, free, with the words "I love you" lingering in your mind.*

ONE LAST, GREAT DATE

BILL VALENTINE

TECHNICALLY, THEY WERE several dates. But, given all that followed, it's not surprising that they have merged in my memory into a single entity. From August 31 to November 11, 2001—one great date.

By the last day of August, the humidity and oppressive heat were gone. The sun was further to the south and the days were getting shorter, making for a perfect late summer evening in New York City. Joe and I had tickets to see Etta James at the B.B. King Blues Club on 42nd Street.

Getting the two of us to a concert—or any event—was never easy. Joe was a flight attendant for American Airlines and his schedule was created anew every month through a complicated bidding process. I had ordered the tickets for Etta early in the summer, in mid-July. Joe put in his bids. Eighteen years of seniority gave him a certain amount of bidding power, but still, we held our breath. This time we were lucky—he got the day off.

I had only discovered Etta the previous summer, when we spent a week on Martha's Vineyard and her "Love's Been Rough on Me" CD played continually in the car. Joe had been a fan for years. She was one of his "ladies"—those female vocalists who stood at the center of his musical universe. They required only one name to be identified: Ella (Fitzgerald), Billie (Holiday), Dinah (Washington), Shirley (Horn), Sarah (Vaughan), and Diana (Krall).

Joe's love of music, and the human voice in particular, came from his mother, Lily. His appreciation of black female vocalists had been nurtured by his older brother, Tony, who produced an album for Faye Carol, a San Francisco cabaret singer. Both were gone now. Lily died in 1980, just a few weeks after Joe and I met. Tony died of AIDS in 1995. Joe loved his ladies for who they were and for their enormous gifts, but I think they also kept him connected to Tony and Lily.

On the 1 train downtown, our thoughts were momentarily diverted from Etta. A young man and woman boarded our car and stood between us, both hanging on to the vertical pole. From their body language it was obvious that sexual energy was passing between them. This was confirmed when I glanced down and noticed a very prominent bulge in the young man's shorts. I looked over to Joe, who was much closer. We each tried to keep a straight face until we got off the train at 42nd Street.

"Was that what I thought it was?" I asked him.

"Oh, my God! I could see the outline of the whole thing pressing against his shorts."

This encounter only fueled our desire to see Etta, high priestess of sensuality. We were taken to our table, where we ordered dinner and a bottle of wine. By the time the opening act was over and Etta had been helped to the stage, the wine was gone. I ordered a second bottle. The review the next day in *The New York Times* would describe a "one woman fortress holding the wisdom of the blues," her voice encompassing "coy teenager and amorous woman, heartbroken lover and spiteful victim, party girl and desperate addict." When she broke into "At Last", she had the whole crowd with her, none more devotedly than Joe. His response to her was intense; when he clapped, he clapped hard, holding his hands up in front of his face, as if he were praying.

I slipped my arm around him; I wanted to be closer to this body from which so much emotion was emanating. Joe had a way of existing in his body that I always envied. I was a bit of a klutz; someone once compared my style of dancing to that of a Boy

Scout marching. Joe was a marvelous dancer. I don't remember which disco song was playing as we took the floor at the End Up in San Francisco, but I will never forget the sight of Joe as he began to dance. He wore a white gauze V-necked Indian shirt. With his mix of Chinese and European features, thick black hair and dark eyes, he looked gorgeous. Each part of his slender body—shoulders, hips, and legs—flowed seamlessly. He danced with the ease of a curtain caught in a gentle wind.

I had known him for just seventy-two hours at that point, but from the beginning I knew that he was different. It wasn't until I saw him dancing, though, that I began to love him. It would not be wrong to say he danced his way into my heart, and my life.

Etta was barely on stage for an hour before she was helped from her chair and escorted off. There would be no encore. We filed out slowly, not wanting to let go of the moment. Outside, there was a buzz on 42nd Street. The sidewalk was crowded with moviegoers, tourists, and others caught up in the excitement of the revitalization of Times Square. We walked the half block back to Broadway and caught the uptown subway.

From the 116th Street station, the blocks to our apartment were downhill and passed quickly. We found ourselves alone in the elevator. Joe was in one corner, I was in another. As we started our ascent, I looked over at him, and flush with the emotions of the evening, I threw myself at him. He was visibly startled (he would die of embarrassment were we to be caught), then he surrendered. We made out passionately until we reached the eighteenth floor. In the apartment, we checked on the cats and went to bed.

Despite the late hour, we plunged into making love. Like any middle-aged couple, our lovemaking had its droughts and ruts. But that night there was an intensity and freshness to it that made me cry out with joy. Finally, we collapsed in exhaustion. It was rare that we were even awake at this hour. We were laughing and shaking our heads as we kissed each other goodnight.

. . . . .

THEN IT WAS September. Sometime early in the morning of the eleventh, Joe arrived back from London and crawled into bed beside me. I was at work in downtown Manhattan when the planes hit. I witnessed the explosion in the south tower from Washington Square Park. When I returned to my office, I tried to call home, but I couldn't get an outside line. A few minutes later, our phone number flashed on my caller ID screen. From the sleepy, innocent texture of his voice, I could tell he didn't know. Barely able to describe what was happening, I finally said, "Turn on the TV."

By mid-afternoon, after the towers had collapsed and the full horror of what we were going through had set in—including the hijacking of two American Airlines planes—I began the long walk back to our apartment. I stopped every half hour to call home from a pay phone. Joe was at the door to greet me. We fell into each other's arms and cried. He had just learned that an old friend had been working on the plane that hit the north tower.

Even though we lived more than six miles from the World Trade Center, on clear nights we could see the twinkling red and green lights of the spoke on the north tower. It was a standing joke that if we sold the apartment we would advertise it as having WTC views. That night, as we stood on our terrace and looked south, all we could see was darkness.

At the end of September, Joe returned to work. Even as we returned to the rituals of daily life, all around us were reminders of the deep trauma and pain that so many others had suffered. I could not walk more than a few yards from my office without seeing a missing person poster. I came to know some by name. I knew what floor they worked on, when they were last seen, and what identifying marks they had.

On October 1, we chose to go out to honor our twenty-first anniversary. In 2000 we had flown out to California to mark the two-decade milestone. This year we would stay close to home. We had a drink at Gotham Bar and Grill, and then dinner at Chez Ma

Tante, a bistro on West 10th Street. It was a quintessential West Village restaurant—cozy, charming, and usually packed with diners. It was empty when we entered. The hostess sat us in a window seat and brought two complimentary glasses of champagne to help us celebrate.

The man sitting across the table from me had finally begun to show signs of aging. Lately there were signs that he was struggling with the realities of middle age. He had had a few minor cosmetic surgeries. He was threatening to dye his hair. He wore it cut short now, to hide the gray. This mattered little to me. So much of my life was different from what I had thought it would be. The exception was our relationship. For more than two decades, Joe had stood at the center of my life; I could not imagine it without him. He was my lover, life partner, and best friend. I looked at him and saw our history together. Not just the good things, abundant as they were, but our struggles, too.

We had created something that was real and enduring. It was there in our bond, but it extended beyond us. It was visible in our circle of friends, many of whom had only known us as a couple. Also in the way in which we each had entered into the other's family, where the next generation had no memory of life without an Uncle Bill or Uncle Joe. It was visible in the home we had built, in the journeys we took, and in the gestures and phrases we employed as a couple. Before there had been two individuals; now there was a third entity. A "we" had been created.

When we left two hours later, Chez Ma Tante was still empty.

At the end of October we flew to Dallas for the wedding of one of Joe's colleagues. After so much tragedy, it was good to attend a happy event associated with American Airlines. The reception was at the hotel where we were staying. Late in the evening, Joe and I hooked up just off the dance floor. We leaned against the wall as we talked, each holding a glass of wine. It was the kind of moment I loved—the evening was winding down, we only had to go upstairs to reach our bed, the wine had created a nice buzz, and for the moment, we found ourselves alone. Suddenly I felt a rush of liquid down the front of my suit. Parts of my shirt, suit jacket, and left pant leg were covered with red. Joe had let his wine glass tip too far forward.

He dashed to find napkins. The situation was hopeless, though. I headed for the elevators. Joe was mortified; he wanted me to change and come back down. I declined; I was tired and we had an early flight. He said he would stay on for a little while longer and then come up. Riding up in the elevator, I found myself grinning. For once Joe, Mr. Smooth, had been the klutz.

. . . . .

OFFEN, THE BEST dates were the simplest ones, the ones when we stayed home. This was how we spent the evening of Sunday, November 11. I was the chef. I bought and prepared the salmon and vegetables. Joe set out olives and opened the wine. He lit the candles, picked out the music, and set the table. We didn't need to discuss these matters any more; they were second nature. I made the salad, but Joe dressed and tossed it. He used a carefully calibrated amount of Ken's Steakhouse Italian Dressing & Marinade. This was the salad dressing I had grown up on; it was like mother's milk to me. But in one of those wonderful twists that occur in relationships, Joe adopted it and it became his dressing.

Joe was flying to Paris that month, but he had put in for an extra trip on Monday. Hoping to get paid without actually flying, he applied for a personal vacation day. After washing the dishes, he retreated to the bedroom to make a phone call. I was sitting at the dining table when he rounded the corner. He had a look of mild disappointment on his face. "I didn't get my PVD," he said. "I have to fly tomorrow. It's just a turn around. I'll be home for dinner." Before he went to bed he wrote out his trip on a piece of paper and hung it on the refrigerator. This was one of the new rules we had adopted after September 11, so I would always know where he was.

There was a part of me that wished he never had to leave,

that had never gotten used to the fact that for him going to work meant getting on an airplane. But I thought little of it. He had come and gone thousands of times. I glanced at the note on the refrigerator before I went to bed. The first line read FLIGHT 587, 8 A.M., JFK TO SANTO DOMINGO.

Flight 587 never made it to Santo Domingo. Just a few moments after taking off from JFK, it crashed in Far Rockaway; all 260 passengers and crewmembers, and five people on the ground, were killed.

. . . . .

THERE IS A tremendous urge to look back and find meaning in events, particularly something as random and brutal as Joe's death. We comfort ourselves by saying he is in a better place; he was too good for this world; he lives on in our hearts. I believe all of the above and none of the above. It is not something we can know.

Do we on some level prepare for our deaths? When Joe spilled his glass of red wine on me was he offering me his blessing? It comforts me to think so. And it comforts me to think of our last few months together as a final stroll through some of the things that were essential to our life as a couple: music, via the Etta James concert; travel, via the trip to Dallas; our home life, via the last night's dinner.

Our last date ended as all great ones should. In the predawn darkness on November 12, he kissed me good-bye and said, "I love you."

ABOUT THE CONTRIBUTORS

ERIC ANDREWS-KATZ has been writing since he could hold a pen. He studied journalism and creative writing at the University of South Florida and eventually moved back to Gainesville where he attended the Florida School of Massage. He has a successful licensed massage practice and currently, with his partner, calls Seattle home. After three years of writing for a Web site (under the name Michael Young), Eric has finished his first book *Magdalene* and his second novel, a spy-parody called *The Jesus Injection*. Two of his short stories will be published in the upcoming anthologies *So Fey: Queer Fairy Fiction* (Haworth) and *Charmed Lives: Gay Spirit in Storytelling* (Lethe Press).

BOB ANGELL was born under a full moon, a telling detail. As a Libran, he is always seeking balance; he rides a unicycle and wishes he could juggle better. You may have seen his work in *Asimov's*, *The Baltimore Review*, *Gargoyle*, and various anthologies. Find him at www.rrangell.com.

VIC BACH lives, works, and writes in New York City. *Kindred Souls*, his debut piece of personal writing, is excerpted and adapted from a larger work, titled *Late Journey Out*.

PHILIP CLARK is a Washington, D.C.-area writer and researcher. His articles and essays have been published in such magazines as *Lambda Book Report* and *The James White Review*. He poetry edited *The William and Mary Review* from 2001-2003 and is currently at work compiling an anthology of poetry by writers who died from AIDS or AIDS-related causes. "The First Waltz" is the first essay from a projected series. He welcomes correspondence at philipclark@hotmail.com.

MICHAEL G. CORNELIUS is the author of the novel *Creating Man* (Vineyard Press, 2001), a Lambda Literary Finalist in 2002, and one of the authors of the popular detective parody series Susan Slutt. He has also published short fiction in numerous journals, magazines, and anthologies.

RYAN FIELD is a thirty-five-year-old freelance writer/editor who lives in Bucks County, PA. His clients include several well-known authors, and his work has been published in commercial anthologies, collections, and periodicals. Among other Web sites, he is a regular contributor to www.bestgayblogs.com and is currently working on a novel.

D J IRELAND lives in a thatched cottage in Buckinghamshire, England, with his cat, Snowy. He studied Music at Oxford University and now works for BBC radio. He is currently writing a novel...

BARRY LOWE is a writer from Sydney, Australia, whose plays have been produced worldwide, including *Homme Fatale: The Joey Stefano Story*, *The Extraordinary Annual General Meeting of the Size-Queen Club*, *The Death of Peter Pan*, *Seeing Things*, and *Rehearsing the Shower Scene from "Psycho."* He also co-wrote the screenplay to *Violet's Visit*. His short stories have appeared in *The Mammoth Book of Gay Erotica*, *Flesh and the Word*, *Boy Meets Boy*, and others. His book on the life and career of Hollywood cult icon Mamie Van Doren will be published in 2007.

MICHAEL LUONGO is a freelance travel writer and photographer, specializing in Latin America and the Middle East. He has been to all seven continents and eighty countries, with Argentina and Afghanistan being his favorites. His work has appeared in *The*

New York Times, the *Chicago Tribune*, *Conde Nast Traveler*, *Bloomberg News*, *Out Traveler*, *Business Traveler*, *National Geographic Traveler*, *PlanetOut* and many other publications. He wrote the *Frommer's Buenos Aires Guide* and edits the Haworth Press *Out in the World* Series on Gay and Lesbian travel literature. His first novel, *The Voyeur*, about a gay sex researcher in the age of Giuliani, will be published by Alyson in early 2007. Visit him at www.michaelluongo.com.

TOM MENDICINO's work has appeared in the three *Best Gay Love Stories* anthologies. He's still celebrating his birthdays with Nick Ifft.

GREGORY L. NORRIS is the author of the baseball-themed gay novel *Hardball* (Alyson) as well as *Ghost Kisses: Gothic Gay Romance Stories* (Leyland Publications). He also worked as a screenwriter on two episodes of Paramount's *Star Trek: Voyager*. For two years he wrote the monthly "Channel News" column for *Sci Fi*, the official magazine of the Sci Fi Channel, and he freelances widely for periodicals such as *Cinescape*, *Soap Opera Update*, *Genesis*, *Smoke*, *Heartland USA*, and others. His stories also appear in *Travelrotica*, *Best Gay Love Stories—NYC*, and *Ultimate Gay Erotica 2007*, among many other anthologies.

STEPHEN OSBORNE is a former improvisational comedian who now toils away in the field of retail management. He lives in Indianapolis, where he can often be spotted trailing behind Jadzia the Wonder Dog, who insists the city is there for her benefit.

ANTHONY PAULL writes a monthly column entitled "The Dating Diet" for Watermark Media, Florida's largest gay and lesbian publication. Currently completing his first novel, Anthony lives in Florida with his partner of five years and their pets. Please visit www.anthonypaull.com.

FRANÇOIS PENEAUD is a teacher, comics critic, and occasional translator who lives in the southwest of France with his partner Michel, whom he thanks for allowing him to write this story. He runs the Gay Comics List (http://gaycomicslist.free.fr) and is hard at work on various graphic novel projects. He's written three short comics for the gay romance online anthology *Young Bottoms in Love*, edited by Tim Fish. The third one will also be included in a print collection of the best of the website that will be published in May 2007

RICK R. REED is the author of the novels *Obsessed*, *Penance*, and *A Face Without a Heart*, and the short story collection, *Twisted: Tales of Obsession and Terror*. In 2007, his novels *IM*, *In the Blood*, and *Deadly Vision: Book One of the Cassandra Chronicles* will be published by Regal Crest Enterprises under their Quest imprint. His short fiction appears in nearly twenty anthologies. He lives in Miami with his partner and is at work on a new novel.

JAY STARRE writes fiction for gay men's magazines such as *Men* and *Torso*. He has also written gay fiction for over thirty-five anthologies, including the *Friction* series, *Travelrotica*, *Ultimate Gay Erotic 2005* and *2006*, *Bear Lust*, and *Full Body Contact*. He lives on English Bay in Vancouver, B.C.

BILL VALENTINE's memoir, *A Season of Grief*, was recently published by Haworth Press. His stories have been published in *Lynx Eye*, *The Marlboro Review*, *South Dakota Review*, *The Baltimore Review*, and *Blithe House Quarterly*, among others.

JIM VAN BUSKIRK's writing has been featured in a variety of books, magazines, newspapers, Web sites, and radio broadcasts. He is co-author of *Gay by the Bay: A History of Queer Culture in the San Francisco Bay Area* and *Celluloid San Francisco: The Film Lover's Guide to Bay Area Movie Locations*. He co-edited the forthcoming anthologies *Identity Envy: Wanting to Be Who We're Not* and *Love, Castro*

Street: Reflections of San Francisco. He is the program manager of the James C. Hormel Gay & Lesbian Center at the San Francisco Public Library.

EZRA REDEAGLE WHITMAN grew up on the Nez Perce Reservation in north central Idaho. He is a serial 'relocator' and many of the stories he writes have to deal with his experiences traveling, moving, or even wandering. He has written and performed for Native American children's theatre, received honors for participation in theatre festivals for dramatic monologues, and published non-fiction in student anthologies. Ezra hopes to become a novelist and will be pursuing graduate studies in creative writing. He currently lives in Grand Forks, North Dakota where he is completing a nursing degree, and enjoys creating mock balance beam routines on the linoleum of his kitchen floor.

MARVIN WEBB spent the last seventeen years as a professional modern dancer in New York City (Martha Graham and Pascal Rioult) and Washington, D.C. (Liz Lerman Dance Exchange). These days, he's not dancing on stage but in offices, organizing payroll and choreographing 401k's. He has a passion for great food and wine and is highly lactose intolerant. This is his first published piece.

ABOUT THE EDITOR

LAWRENCE SCHIMEL is a full-time author and anthologist who's published over eighty books, including *Two Boys in Love*, *The Future is Queer*, *The Drag Queen of Elfland*, *Kosher Meat*, *Things Invisible to See: Lesbian and Gay Tales of Magic Realism*, *Two Hearts Desire: Gay Couples on their Love*, *The Mammoth Book of Gay Erotica*, and *Vacation in Ibiza*, among others. His *PoMoSexuals: Challenging Assumptions about Gender and Sexuality* (with Carol Queen) won a Lambda Literary Award in 1998, and he has also been a finalist for the Lambda Literary Award ten other times. The German edition of his anthology *Switch Hitters: Lesbians Write Gay Male Erotica and Gay Men Write Lesbian Erotica* (with Carol Queen) won the Siegesseuele Best Book of the Year Award. He won the Rhysling Award for Poetry in 2002 and his children's book *No hay nada como el original* (illustrated by Sara Rojo Pérez) was selected by the International Youth Library in Munich for the White Ravens 2005. He has also been a finalist for the Firecracker Alternative Book Award (twice), the Small Press Book Award (twice), and the Spectrum Award (twice). His work has been widely anthologized in *The Random House Book of Science Fiction Stories*, *The Best of Best Gay Erotica*, *The Mammoth Book of Gay Short Stories*, *Chicken Soup for the Horse-Lover's Soul 2*, and *The Random House Treasury of Light Verse*, among many others. His writings have been translated into Basque, Catalan, Croatian, Czech, Dutch, Esperanto, Finnish, French, Galician, German, Greek, Hungarian, Indonesian, Italian, Japanese, Polish, Portuguese, Romanian, Russian, Slovak, and Spanish. For two years he served as co-chair of the Publishing Triangle, the organization of lesbians and gay men in the publishing industry, and he also served as the regional advisor of the Spain Chapter of the Society of Children's Book Writers and Illustrators for five years. Born in New York City in 1971, he lives in Madrid, Spain.